BINKY

TO THE RESCUE

KIDS CAN PRESS

To Jared, for living with me during the creation of this book

Kids Can Press acknowledges the financial support of the Government of Ontario, through the Ontario Media Development Corporation's Ontario Book Initiative; the Ontario Arts Council; the Canada Council for the Arts; and the Government of Canada, through the CBF, for our publishing activity.

Published in Canada by
Kids Can Press Ltd.
25 Dockside Drive
Toronto, ON M5A 0B5

Published in the U.S. by
Kids Can Press Ltd.
2250 Military Road
Tonawanda, NY 14150

www.kidscanpress.com

The artwork in this book was rendered in ink, watercolor, cat fur and bits of kitty litter.
The text is set in Fontoon.

Edited by Tara Walker
Designed by Karen Powers

The hardcover edition of this book is smyth sewn casebound.
The paperback edition of this book is limp sewn with a drawn-on cover.
Manufactured in Shen Zhen, Guang Dong, P.R. China, in 8/2013 by Printplus Limited

CM 10 0 9 8 7 6 5 4 3 2
CM PA 10 0 9 8 7 6 5 4 3

Library and Archives Canada Cataloguing in Publication

Spires, Ashley, 1978–
Binky to the rescue / by Ashley Spires.

(A Binky adventure)
For ages 7–10.

ISBN 978-1-55453-502-6 (bound) ISBN 978-1-55453-597-2 (pbk.)

I. Title. II. Series: Spires, Ashley, 1978– . Binky adventure.
PS8637.P57B553 2010 jC813'.6 C2009-906866-4

Kids Can Press is a Corus™ Entertainment company

We at W.A.S.P. (Wasps Against Stereotypes and Propaganda) in no way endorse BINKY TO THE RESCUE. By portraying wasps as villains, this story is ignoring the years of anger management counseling and diligent charity work in which many wasps have engaged. Be a friend to wasps: don't read this book.

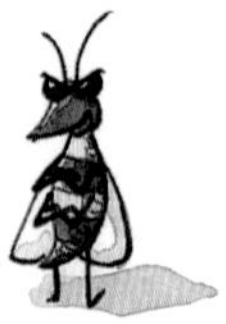

BINKY
TO THE RESCUE
by ASHLEY SPIRES

bzzzzzz

ANOTHER ONE GOT IN.

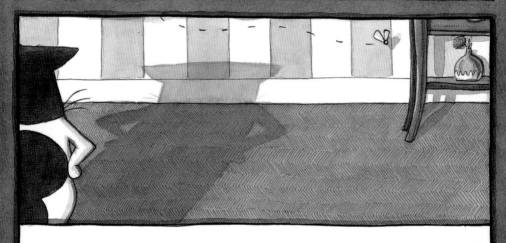

IT'S THE THIRD ALIEN TODAY.

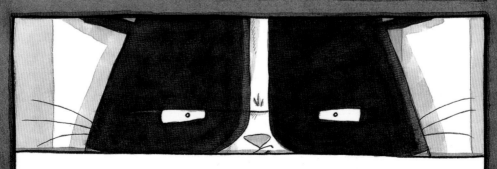

BUT IT WILL NOT ESCAPE.

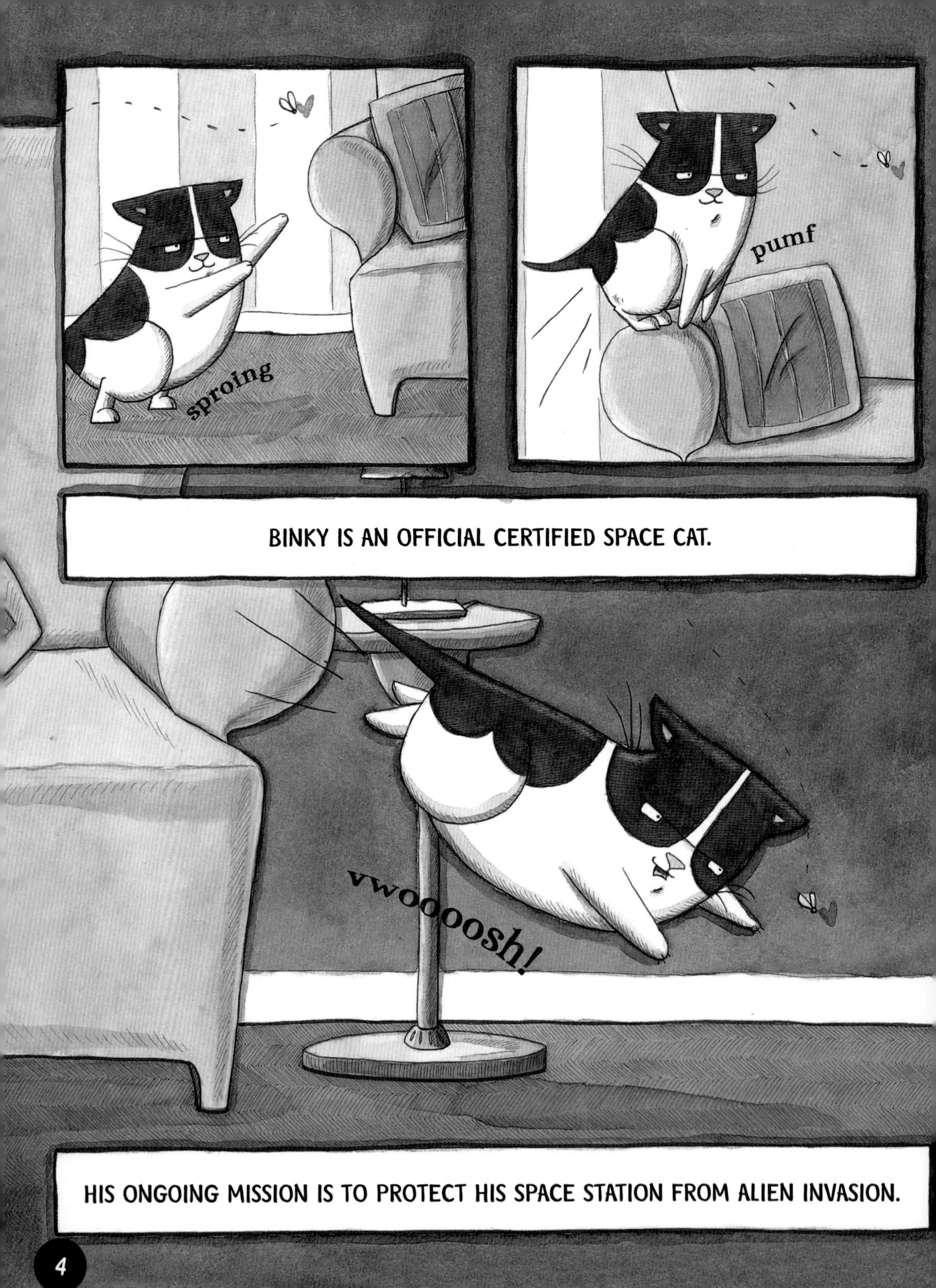
sproing
pumf
BINKY IS AN OFFICIAL CERTIFIED SPACE CAT.
vwoooosh!
HIS ONGOING MISSION IS TO PROTECT HIS SPACE STATION FROM ALIEN INVASION.

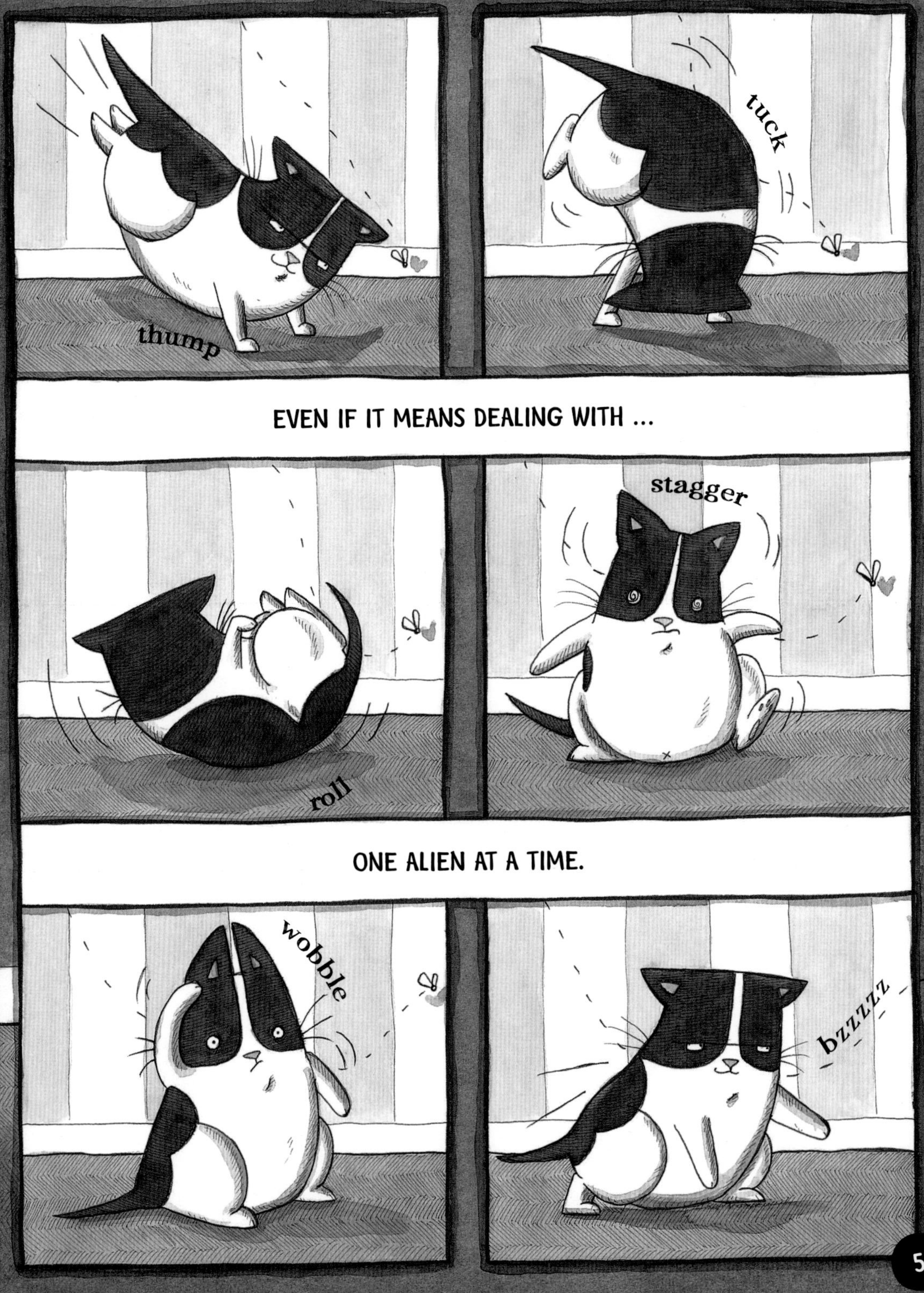
thump
tuck
EVEN IF IT MEANS DEALING WITH ...
roll
stagger
ONE ALIEN AT A TIME.
wobble
bzzzzz

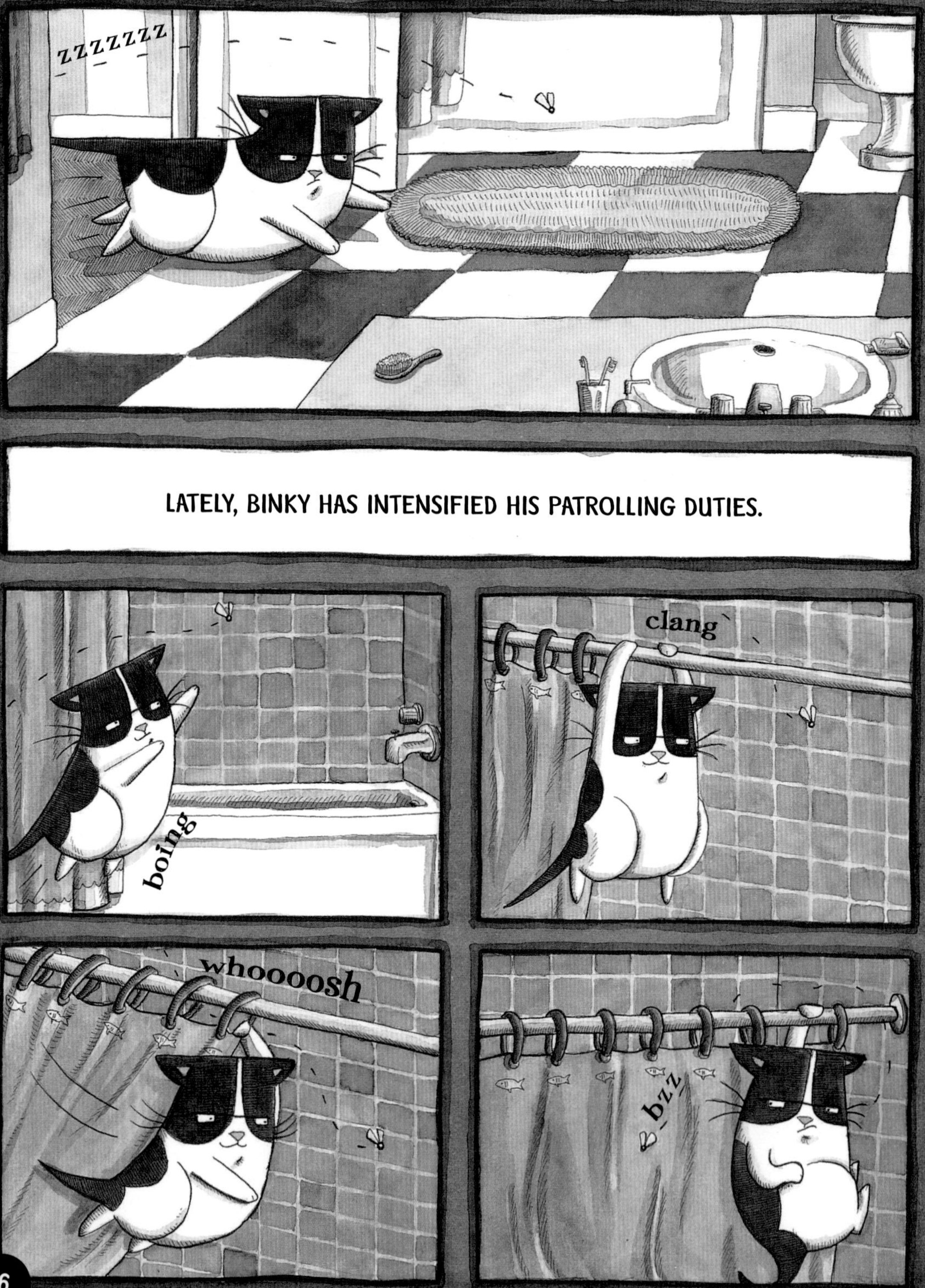
zzzzzzz
LATELY, BINKY HAS INTENSIFIED HIS PATROLLING DUTIES.
boing
clang
whooooosh
bzz

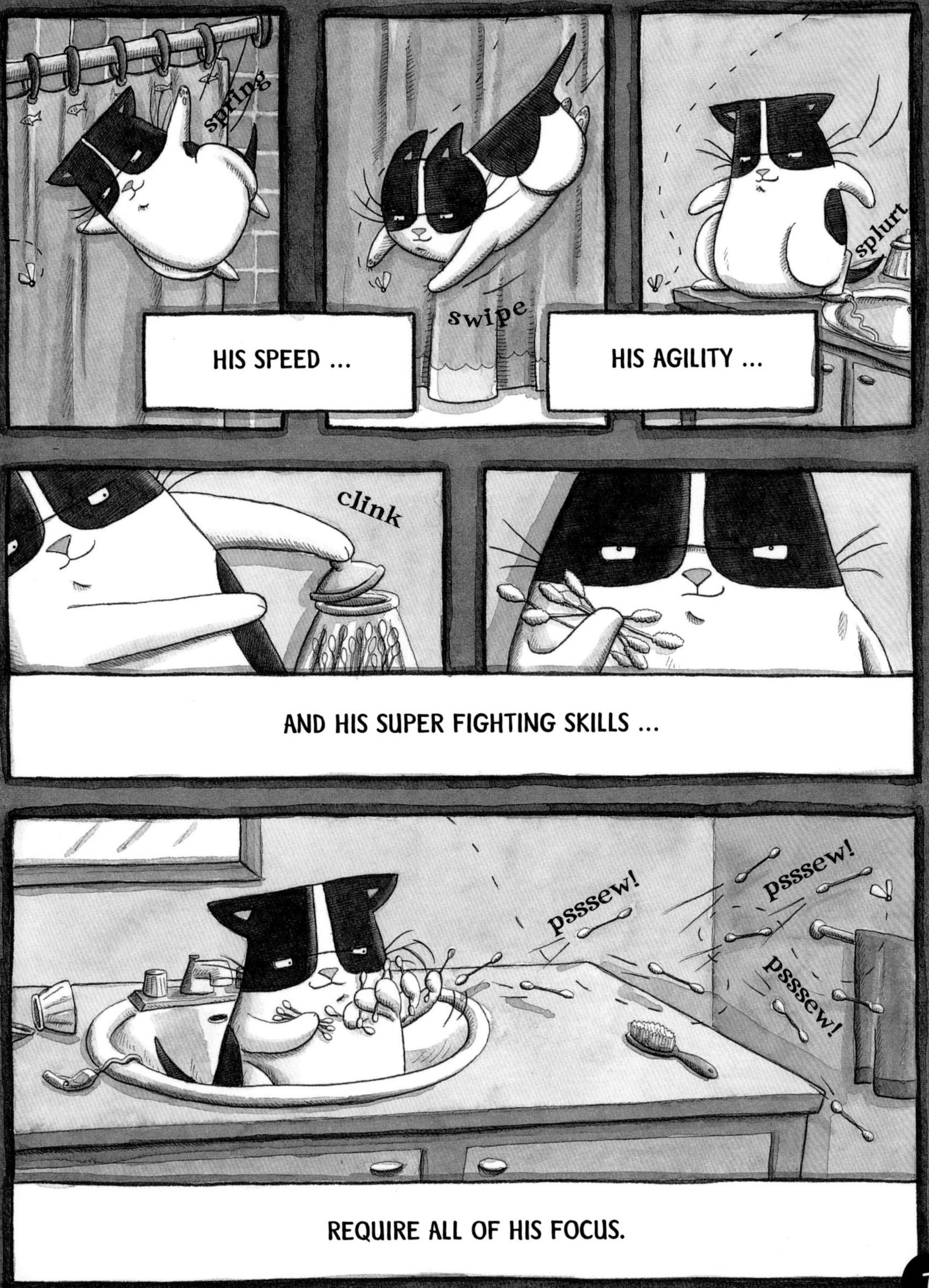
spring
HIS SPEED ...
swipe
splurt
HIS AGILITY ...
clink
AND HIS SUPER FIGHTING SKILLS ...
psssew!
psssew!
psssew!
REQUIRE ALL OF HIS FOCUS.

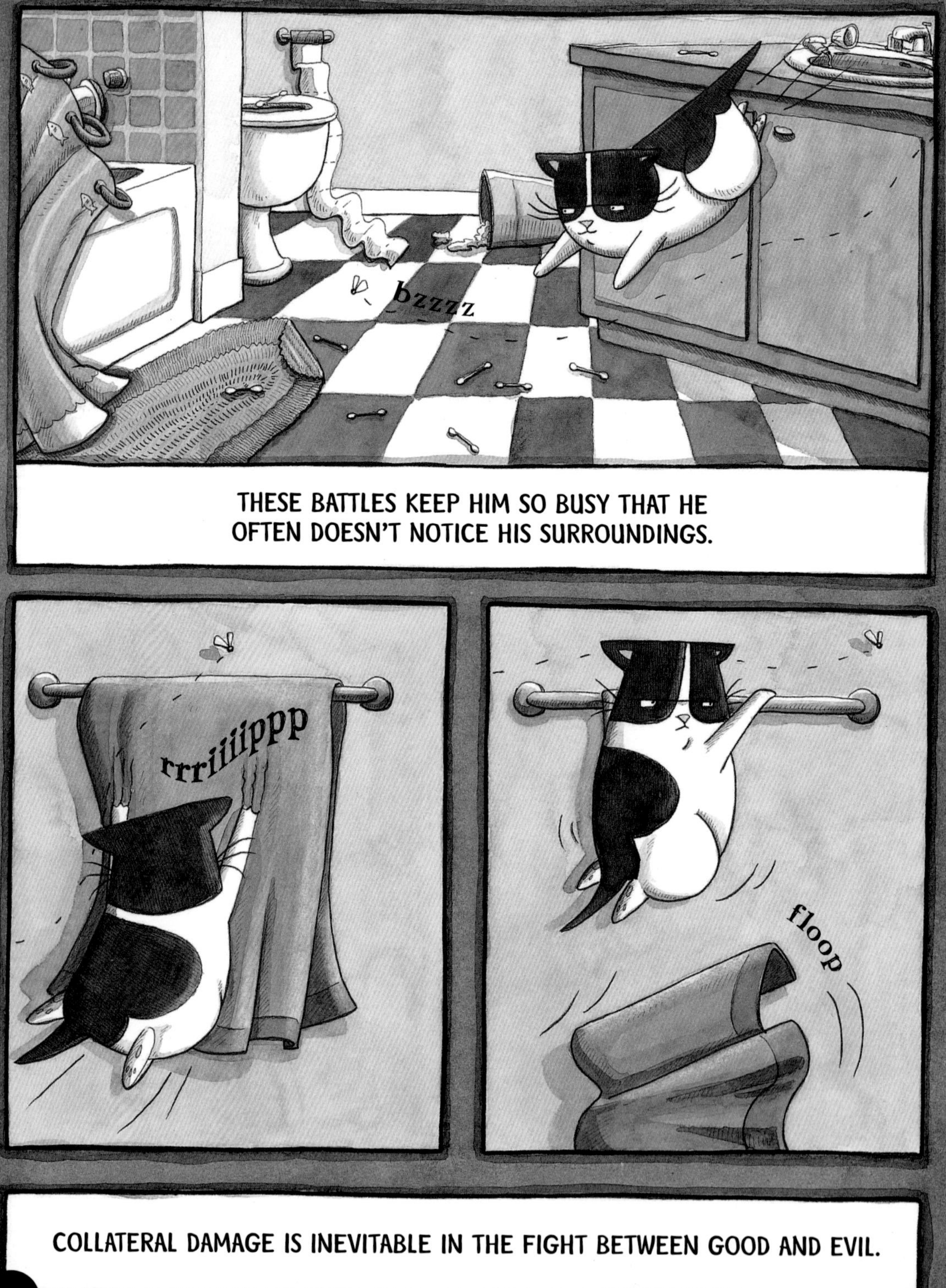
bzzzz
THESE BATTLES KEEP HIM SO BUSY THAT HE OFTEN DOESN'T NOTICE HIS SURROUNDINGS.
rrriiiippp
floop
COLLATERAL DAMAGE IS INEVITABLE IN THE FIGHT BETWEEN GOOD AND EVIL.

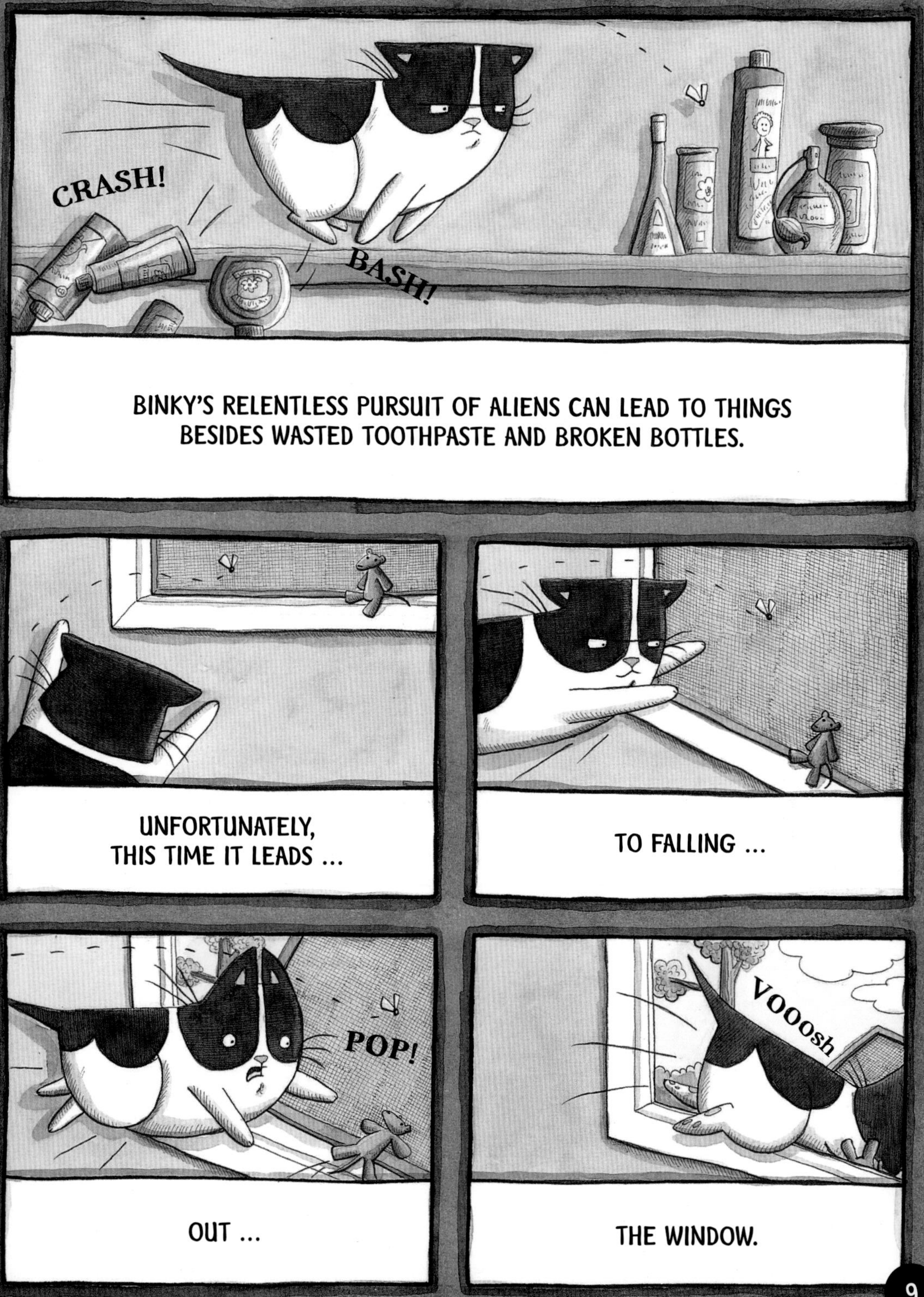
CRASH!
BASH!
BINKY'S RELENTLESS PURSUIT OF ALIENS CAN LEAD TO THINGS BESIDES WASTED TOOTHPASTE AND BROKEN BOTTLES.
UNFORTUNATELY, THIS TIME IT LEADS ...
TO FALLING ...
POP!
OUT ...
VOOOsh
THE WINDOW.

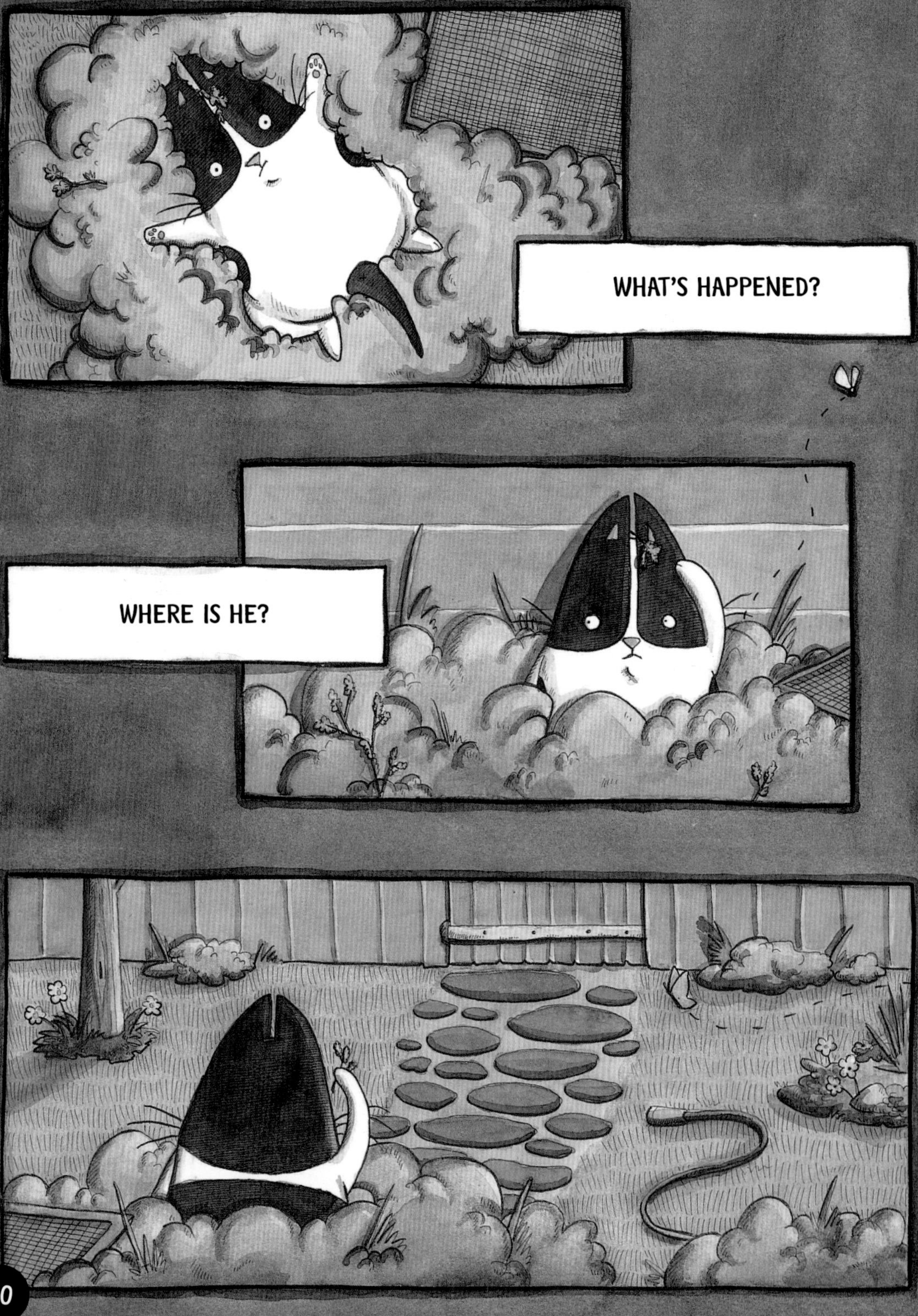
WHAT'S HAPPENED?
WHERE IS HE?

HOLY FUZZBUTT!

BINKY IS IN **OUTER SPACE!!!**

swoosh!

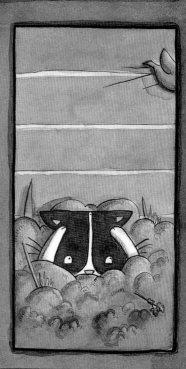

FOR THE FIRST TIME EVER, HE IS OUTSIDE OF HIS SPACE STATION.

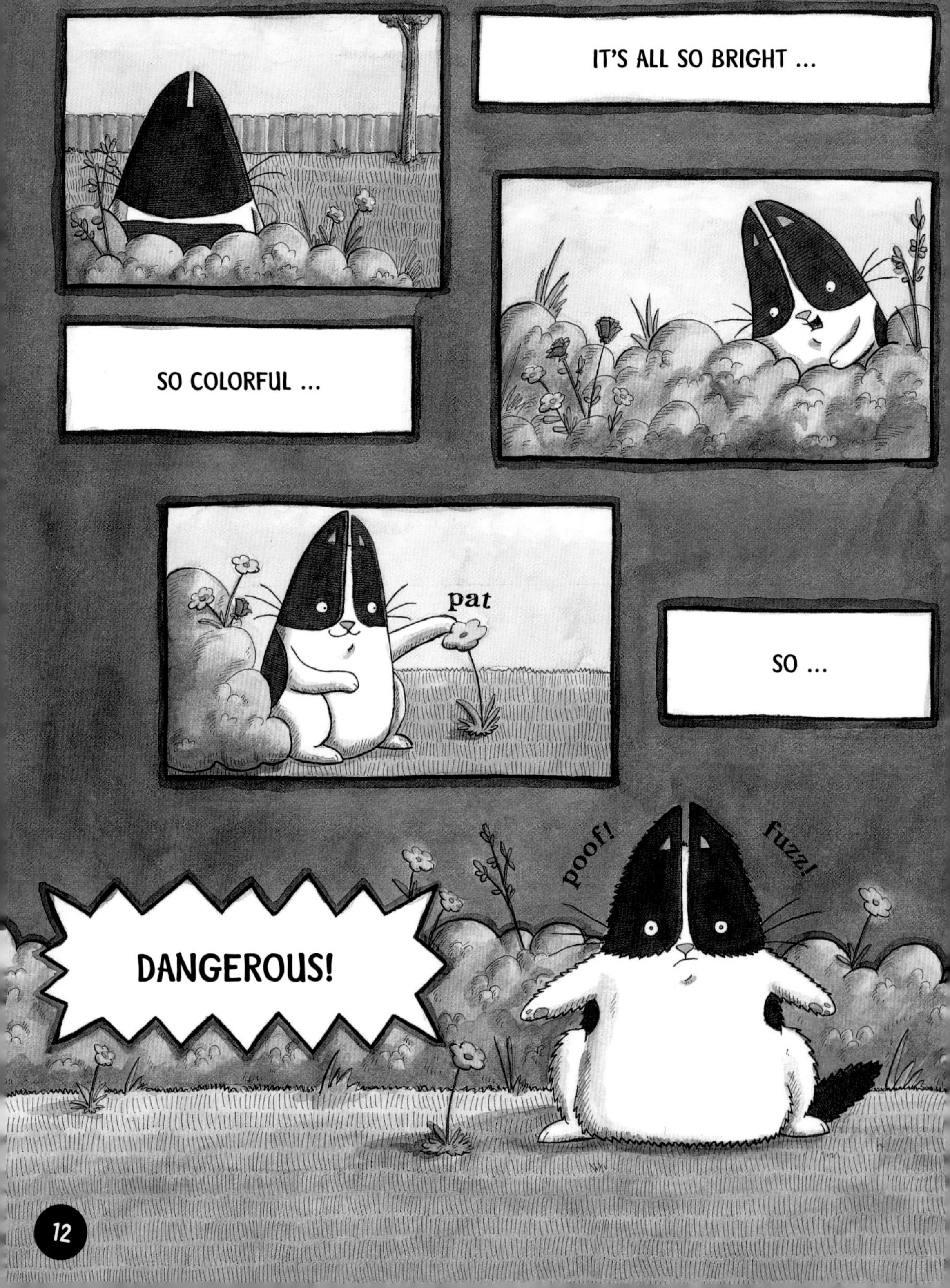
IT'S ALL SO BRIGHT ...
SO COLORFUL ...
pat
SO ...
DANGEROUS!
poof!
fuzz!

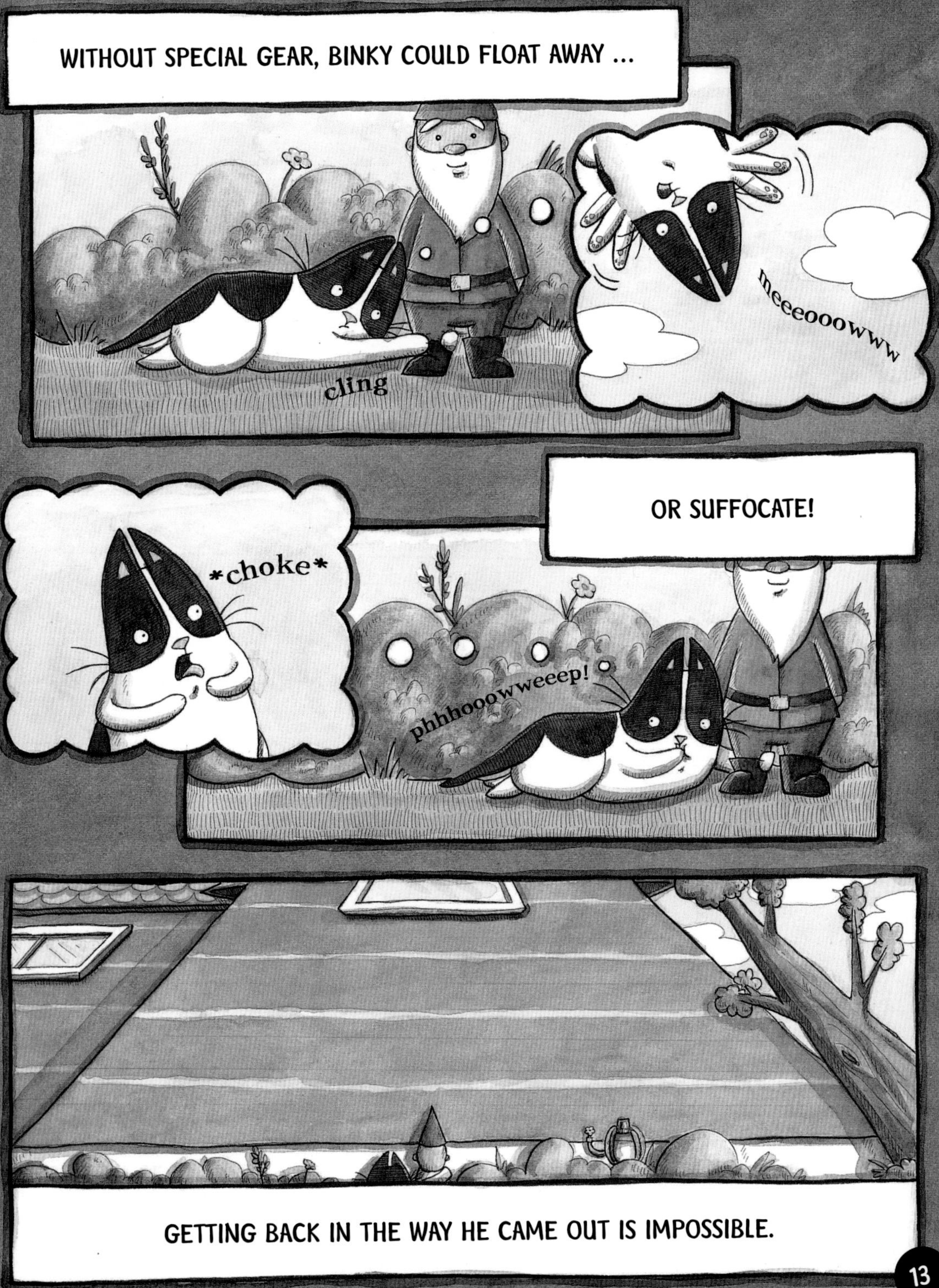
WITHOUT SPECIAL GEAR, BINKY COULD FLOAT AWAY ...
cling
meeeooowwww
OR SUFFOCATE!
choke
phhhooowweeep!
GETTING BACK IN THE WAY HE CAME OUT IS IMPOSSIBLE.

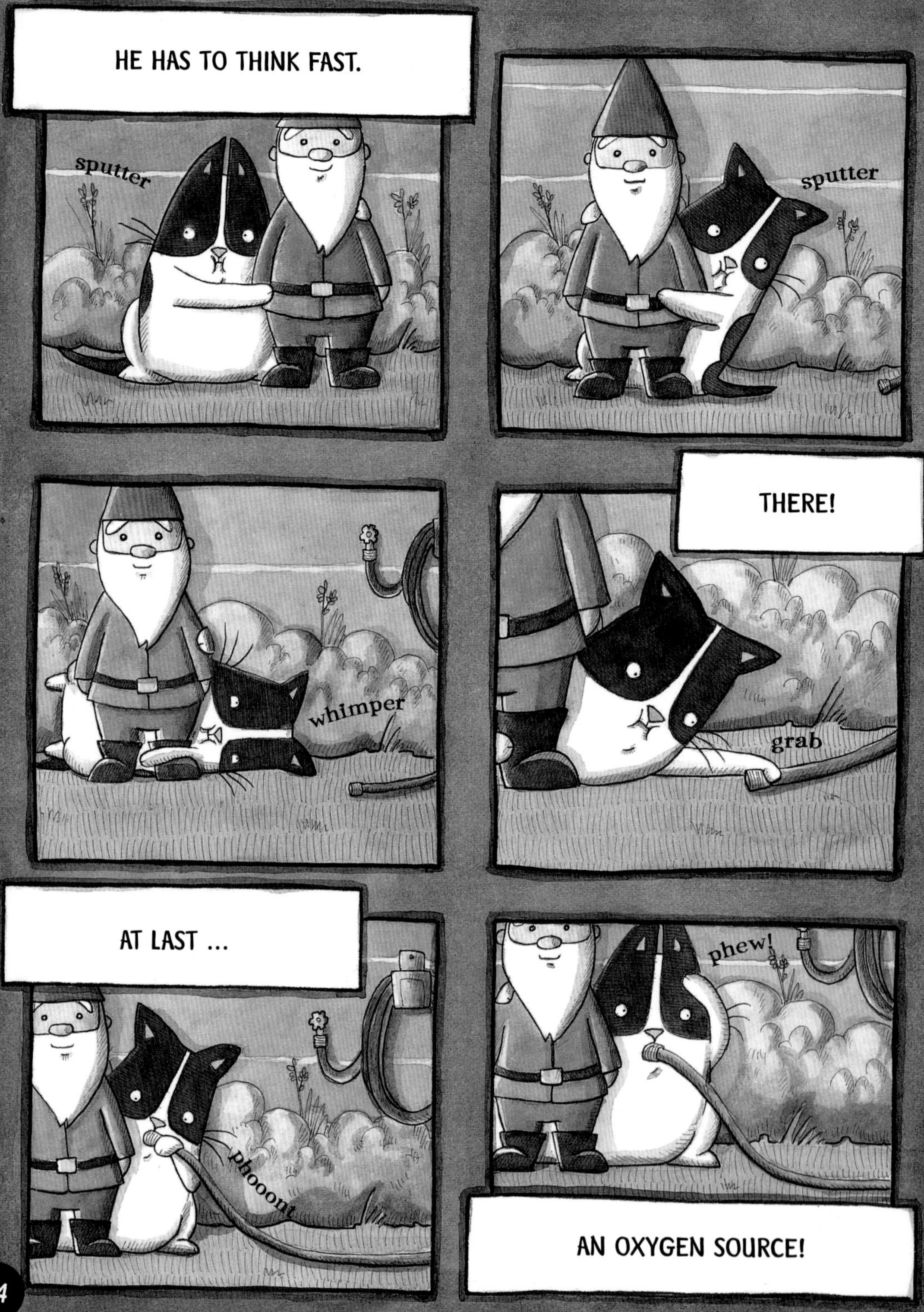
HE HAS TO THINK FAST.
sputter
sputter
whimper
THERE!
grab
AT LAST ...
phooont
phew!
AN OXYGEN SOURCE!

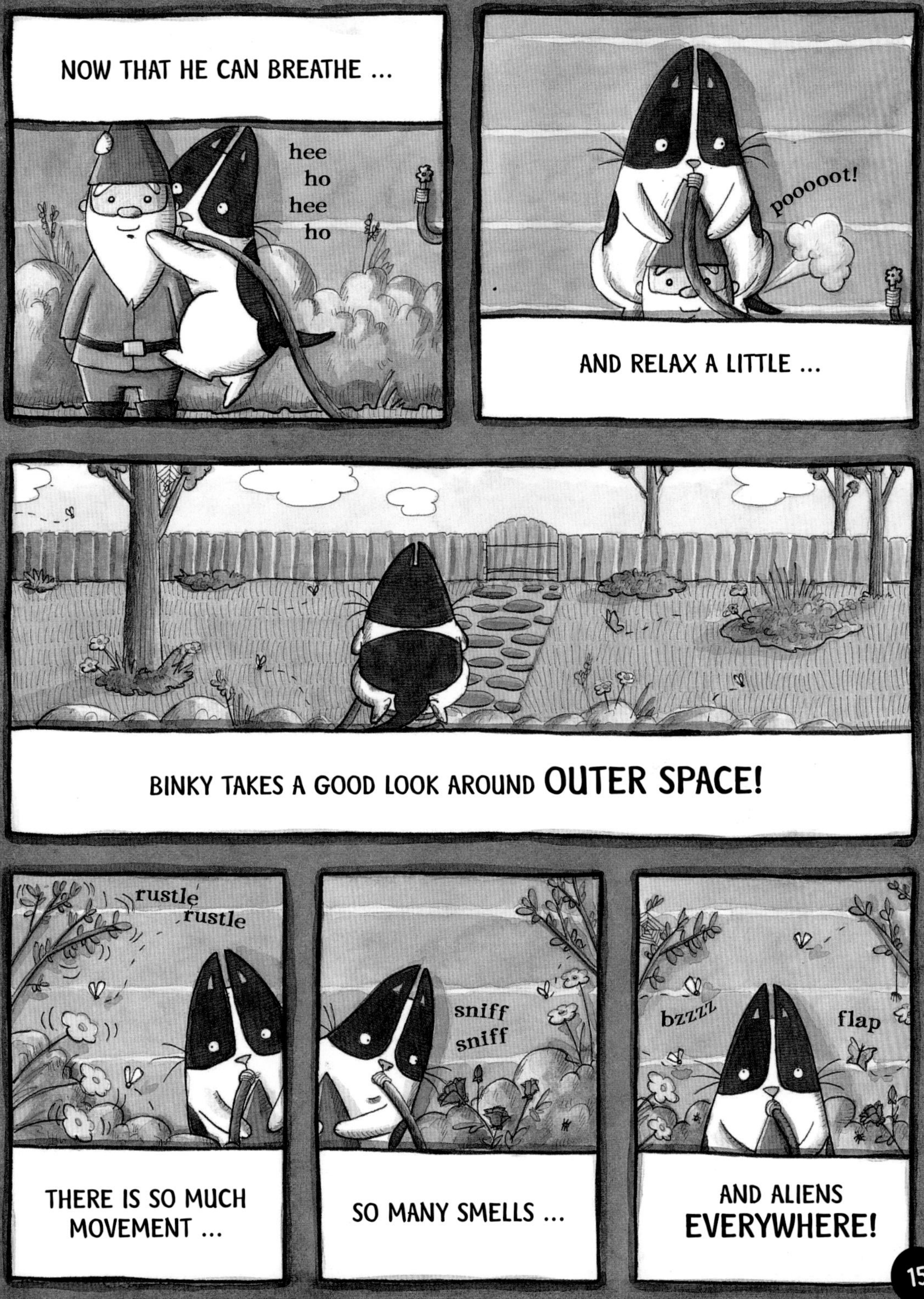
NOW THAT HE CAN BREATHE ...
hee
ho
hee
ho
pooooot!
AND RELAX A LITTLE ...
BINKY TAKES A GOOD LOOK AROUND OUTER SPACE!
rustle
rustle
THERE IS SO MUCH MOVEMENT ...
sniff
sniff
SO MANY SMELLS ...
bzzzz
flap
AND ALIENS EVERYWHERE!

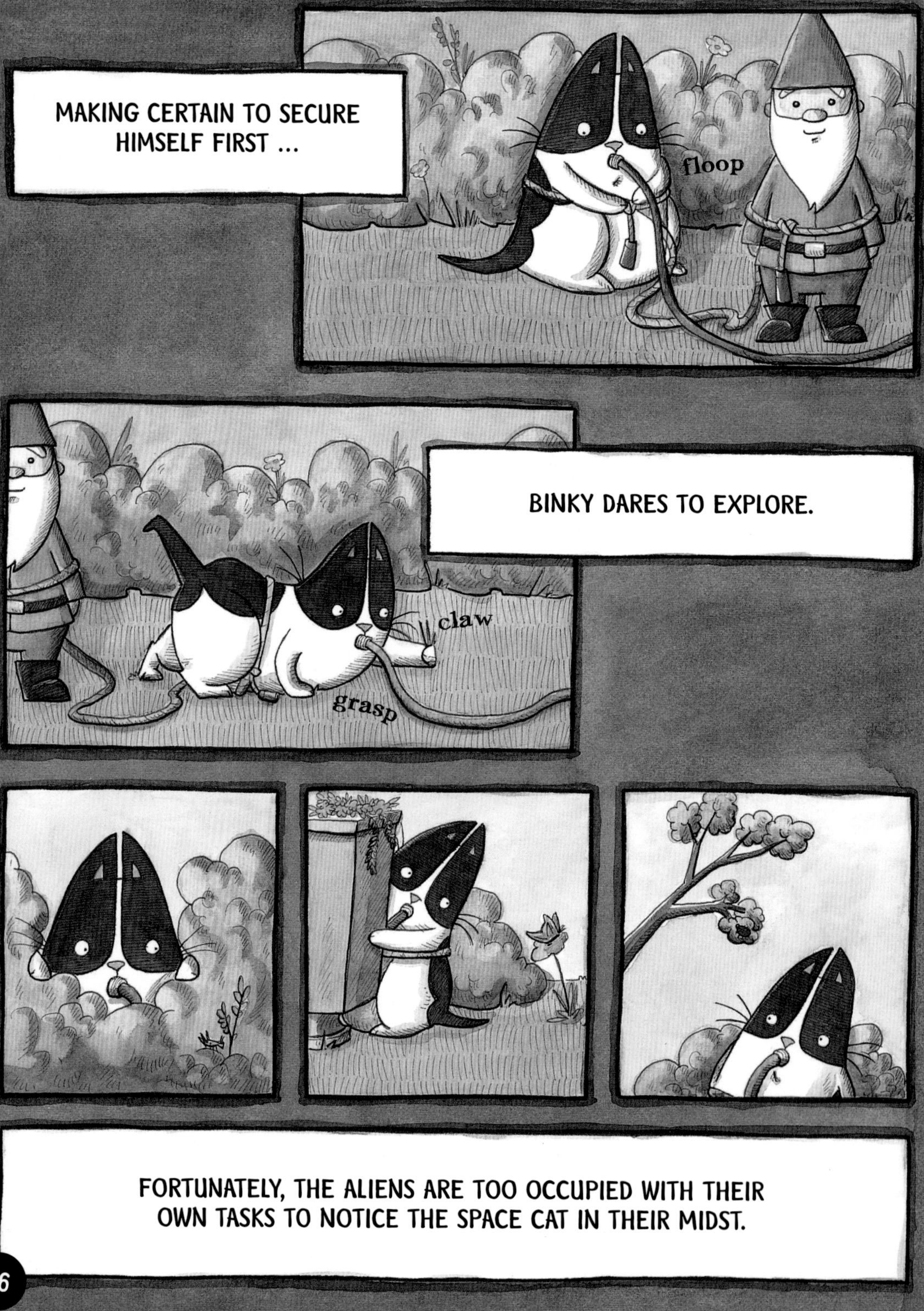
MAKING CERTAIN TO SECURE HIMSELF FIRST ...
floop
BINKY DARES TO EXPLORE.
claw
grasp
FORTUNATELY, THE ALIENS ARE TOO OCCUPIED WITH THEIR OWN TASKS TO NOTICE THE SPACE CAT IN THEIR MIDST.

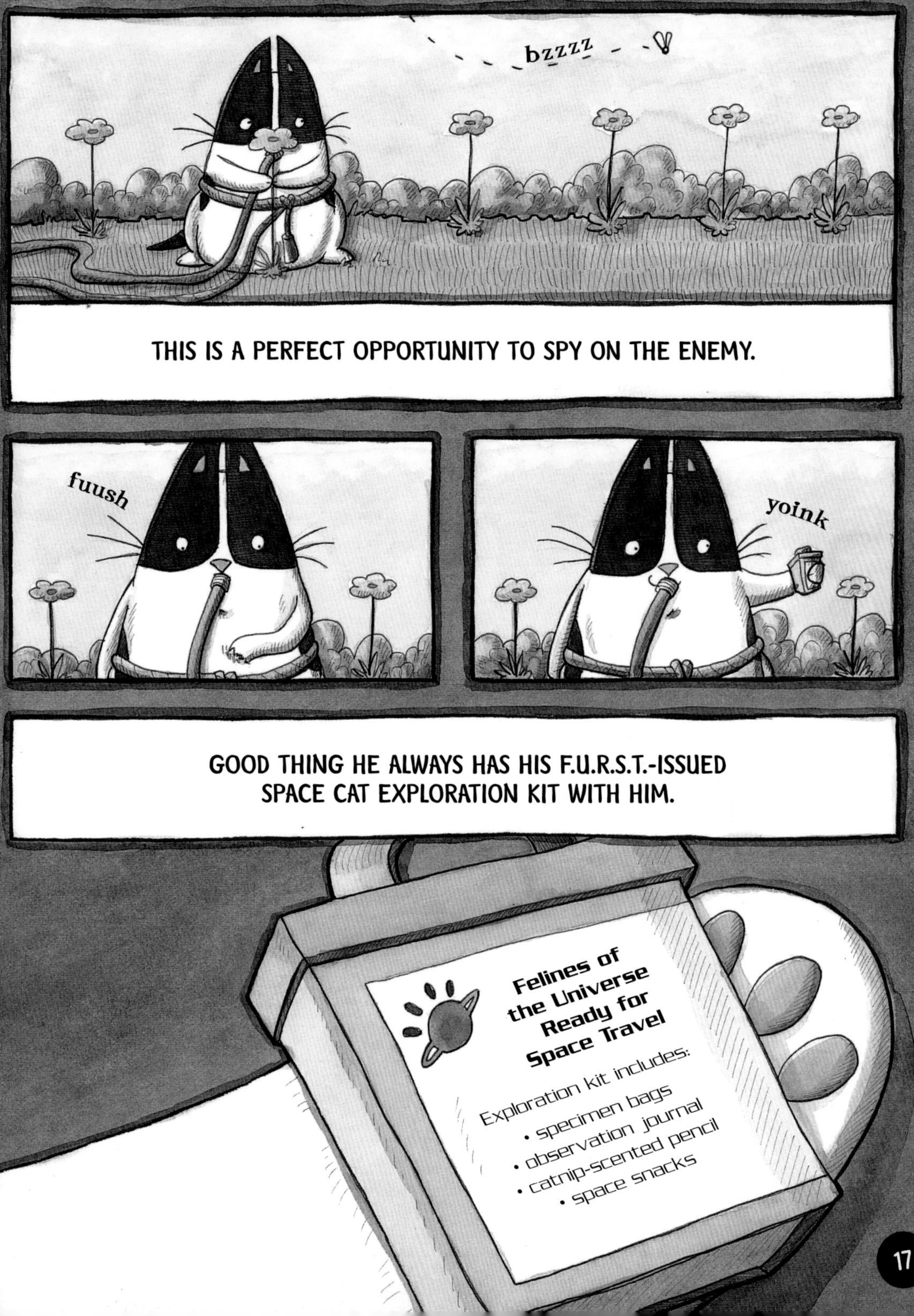
bzzzz
THIS IS A PERFECT OPPORTUNITY TO SPY ON THE ENEMY.
fuush
yoink
GOOD THING HE ALWAYS HAS HIS F.U.R.S.T.-ISSUED SPACE CAT EXPLORATION KIT WITH HIM.
Felines of the Universe Ready for Space Travel
Exploration kit includes:
• specimen bags
• observation journal
• catnip-scented pencil
• space snacks

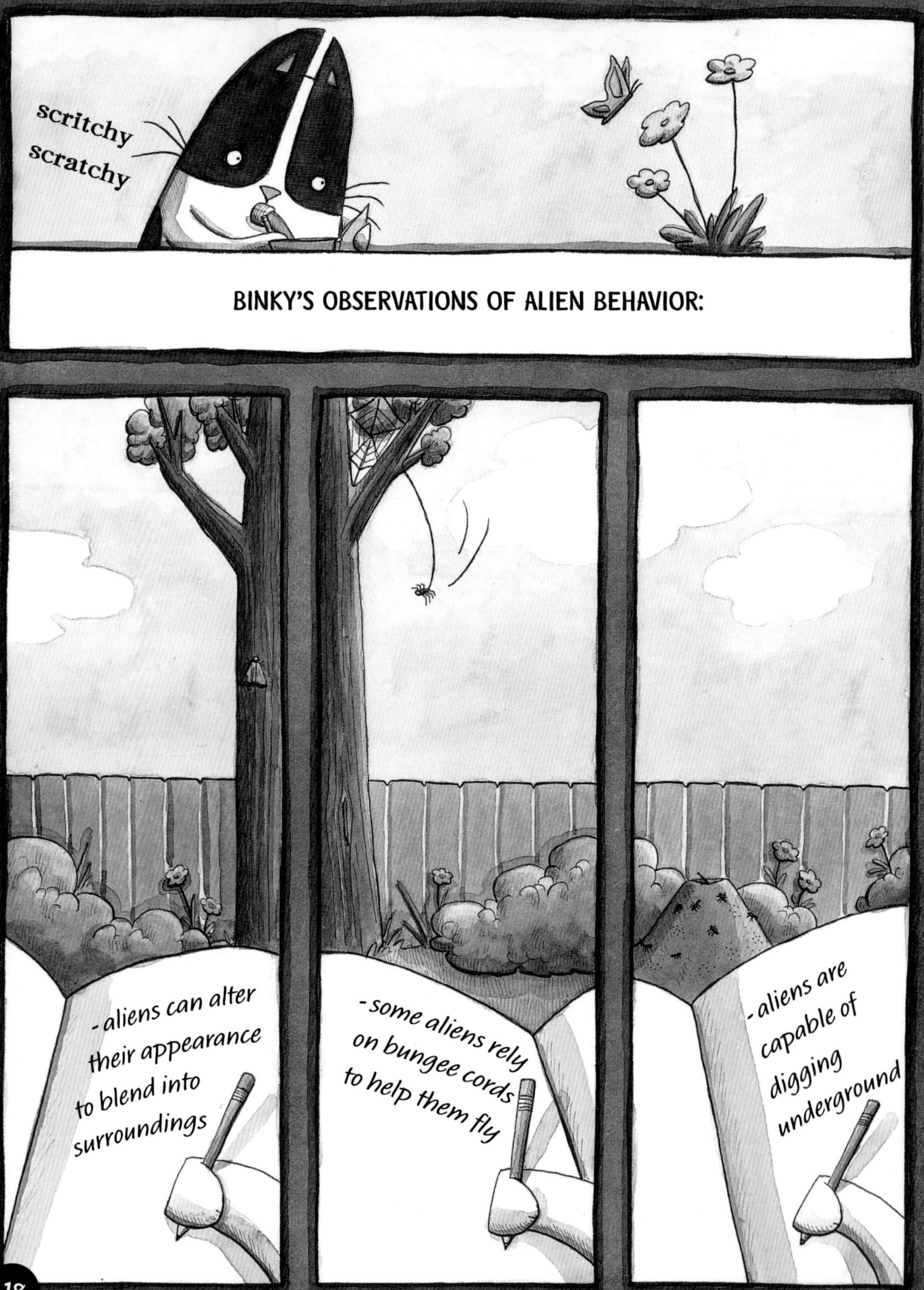

scritchy
scratchy
BINKY'S OBSERVATIONS OF ALIEN BEHAVIOR:
- aliens can alter their appearance to blend into surroundings
- some aliens rely on bungee cords to help them fly
- aliens are capable of digging underground

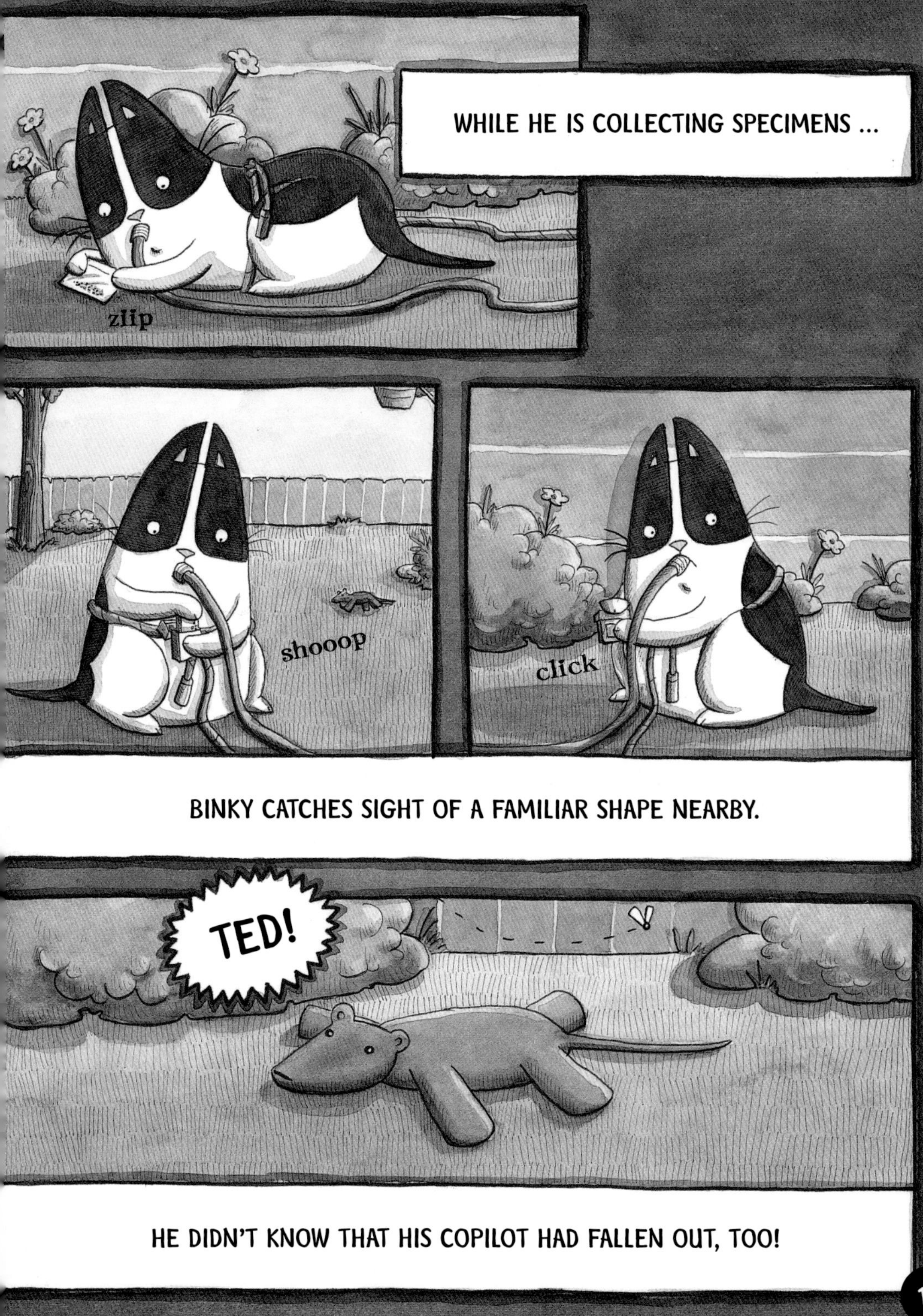
WHILE HE IS COLLECTING SPECIMENS ...
zlip
shooop
click
BINKY CATCHES SIGHT OF A FAMILIAR SHAPE NEARBY.
TED!
HE DIDN'T KNOW THAT HIS COPILOT HAD FALLEN OUT, TOO!

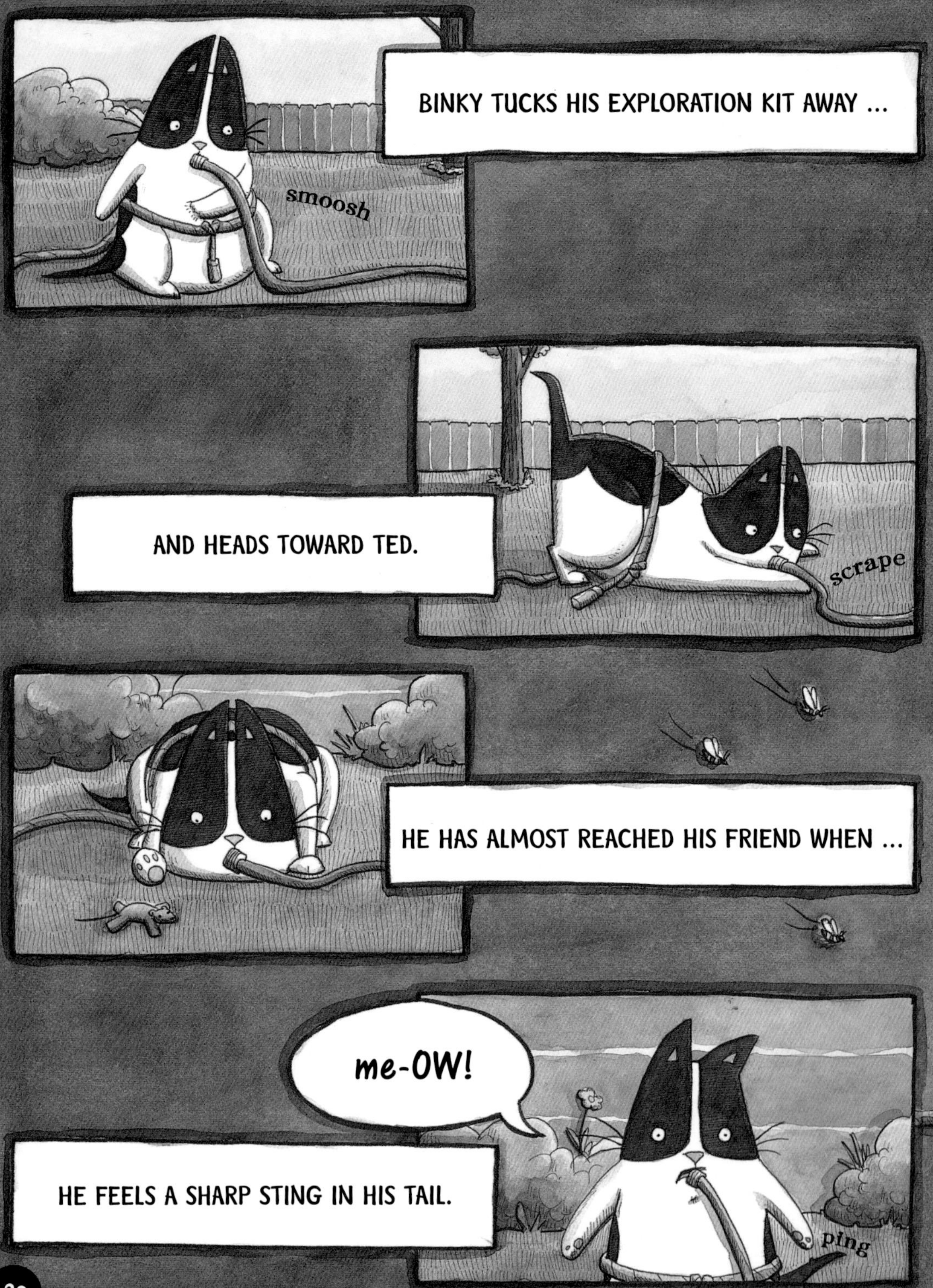
BINKY TUCKS HIS EXPLORATION KIT AWAY ...
smoosh
AND HEADS TOWARD TED.
scrape
HE HAS ALMOST REACHED HIS FRIEND WHEN ...
me-OW!
HE FEELS A SHARP STING IN HIS TAIL.
ping

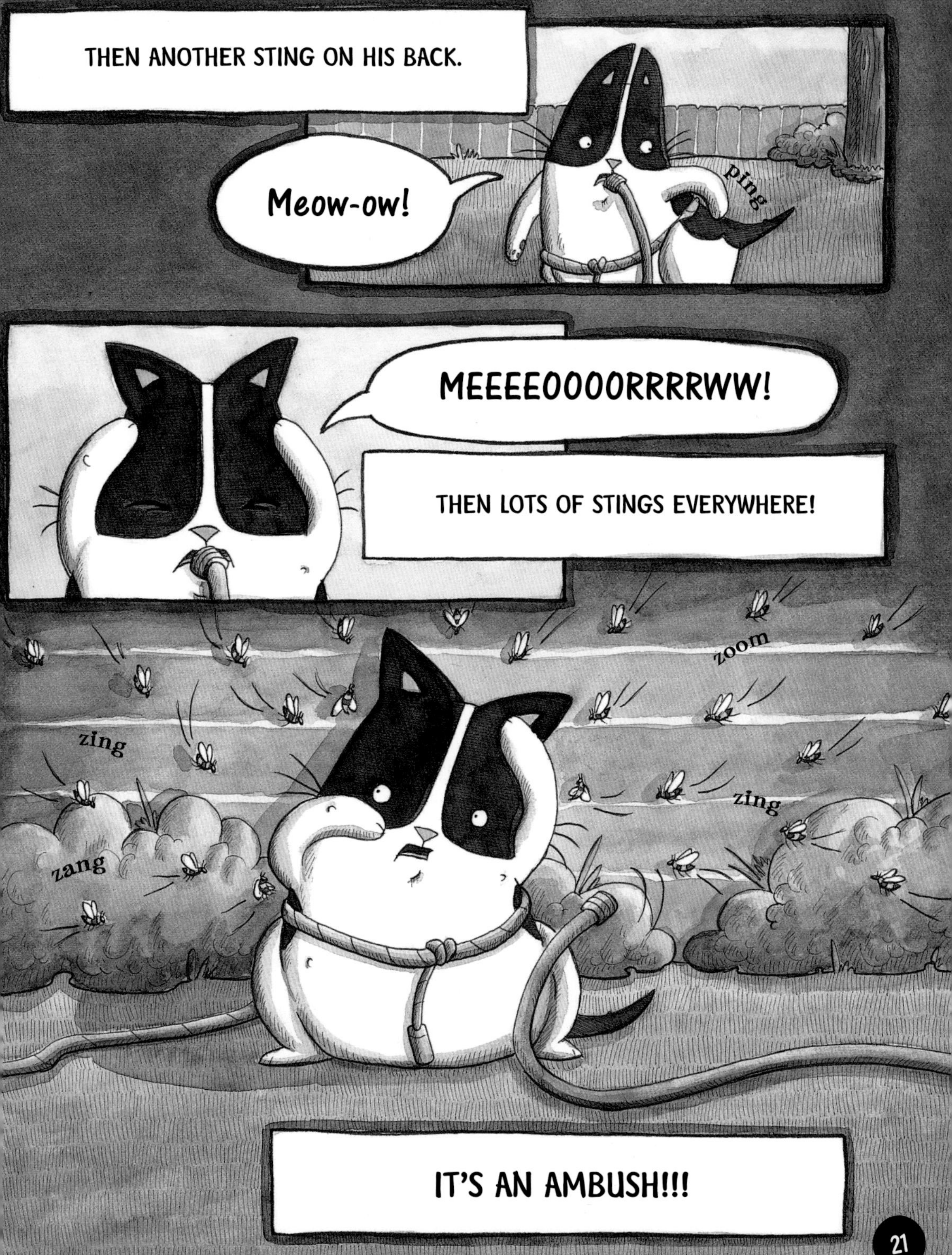
THEN ANOTHER STING ON HIS BACK.
Meow-ow!
ping
MEEEEOOOORRRRWW!
THEN LOTS OF STINGS EVERYWHERE!
zoom
zing
zing
zang
IT'S AN AMBUSH!!!

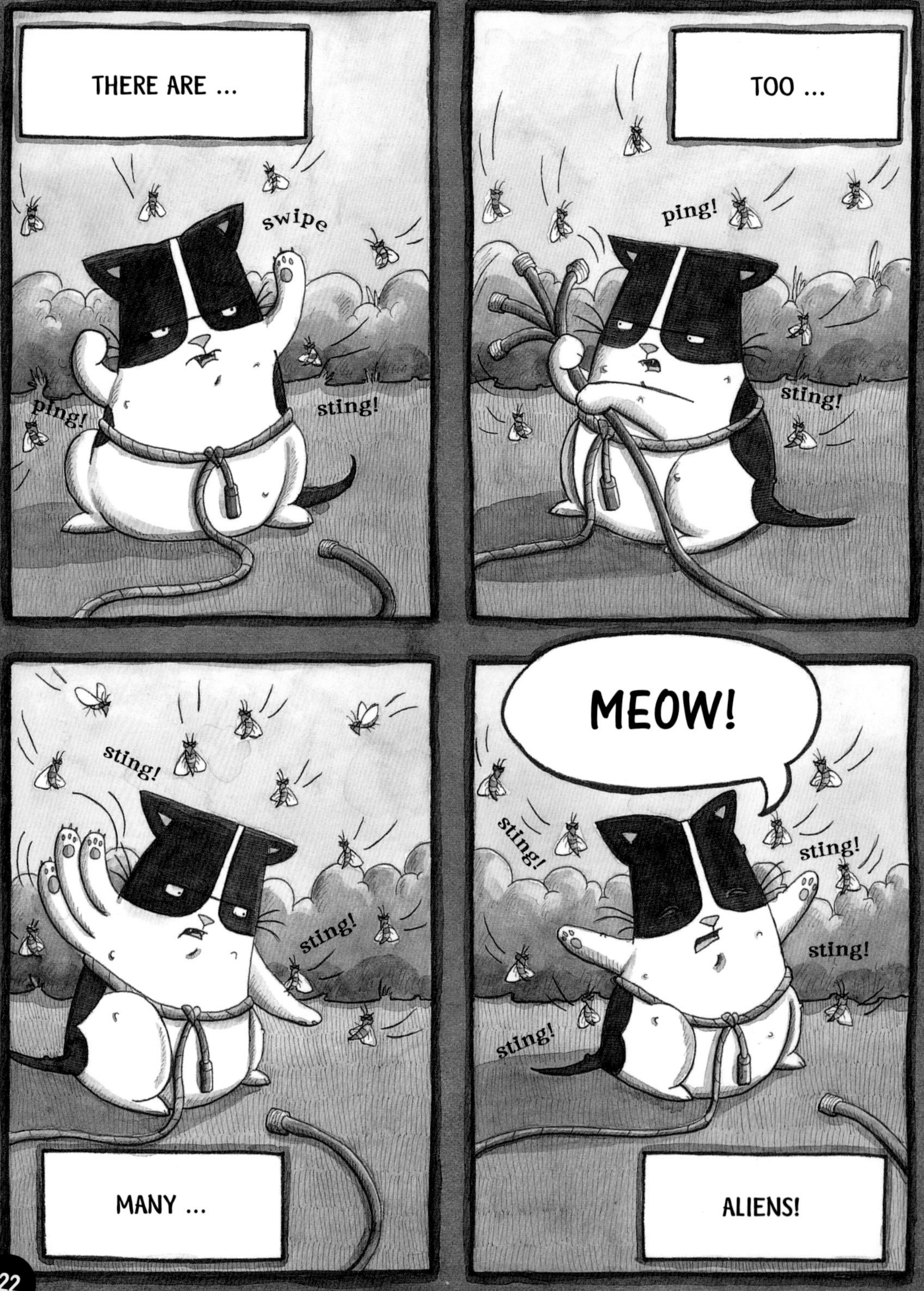
THERE ARE ...
swipe
ping!
sting!
TOO ...
ping!
sting!
sting!
sting!
MANY ...
MEOW!
sting!
sting!
sting!
sting!
ALIENS!

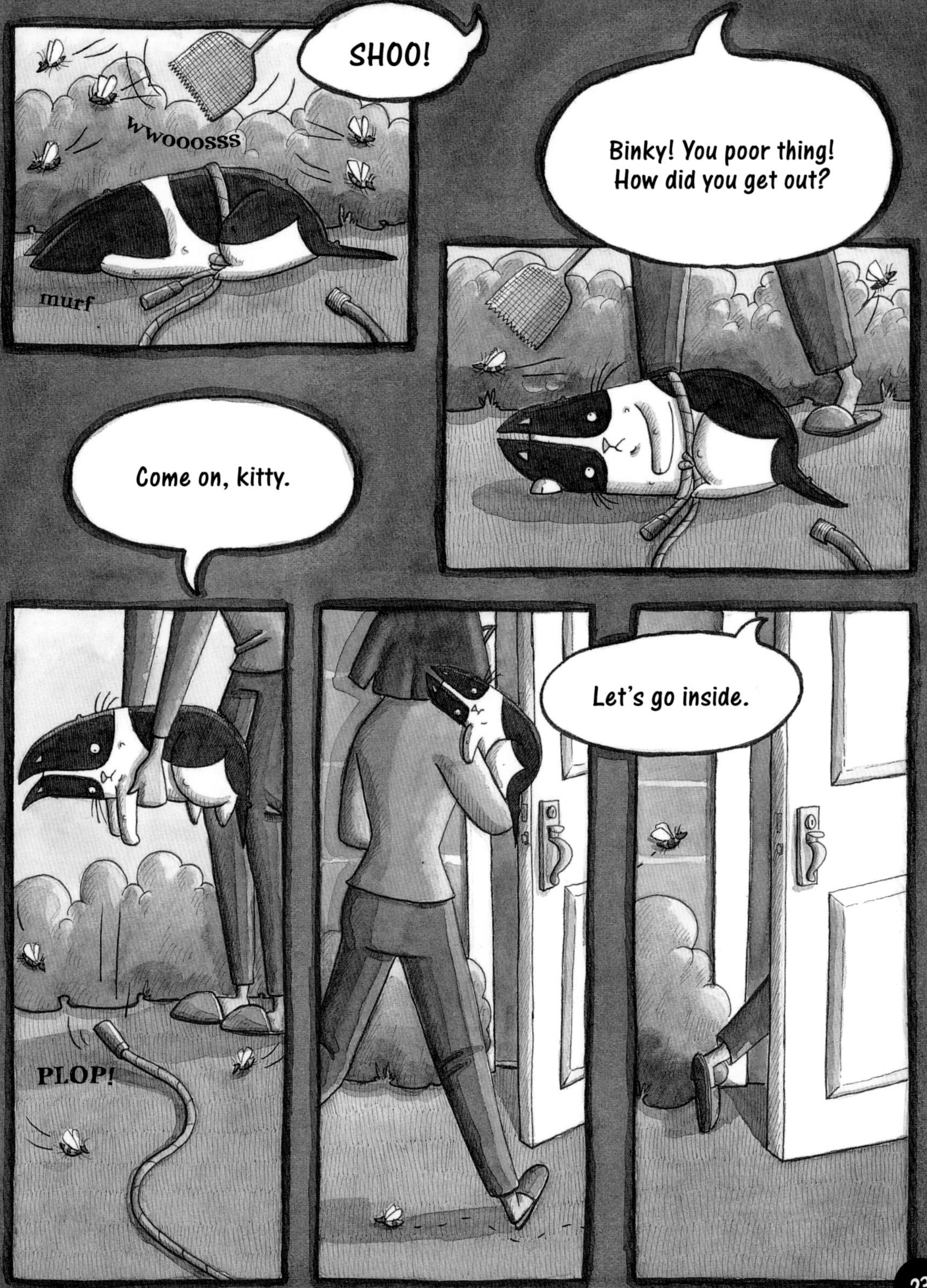
SHOO!
WWOOOSSS
murf
Binky! You poor thing! How did you get out?
Come on, kitty.
PLOP!
Let's go inside.

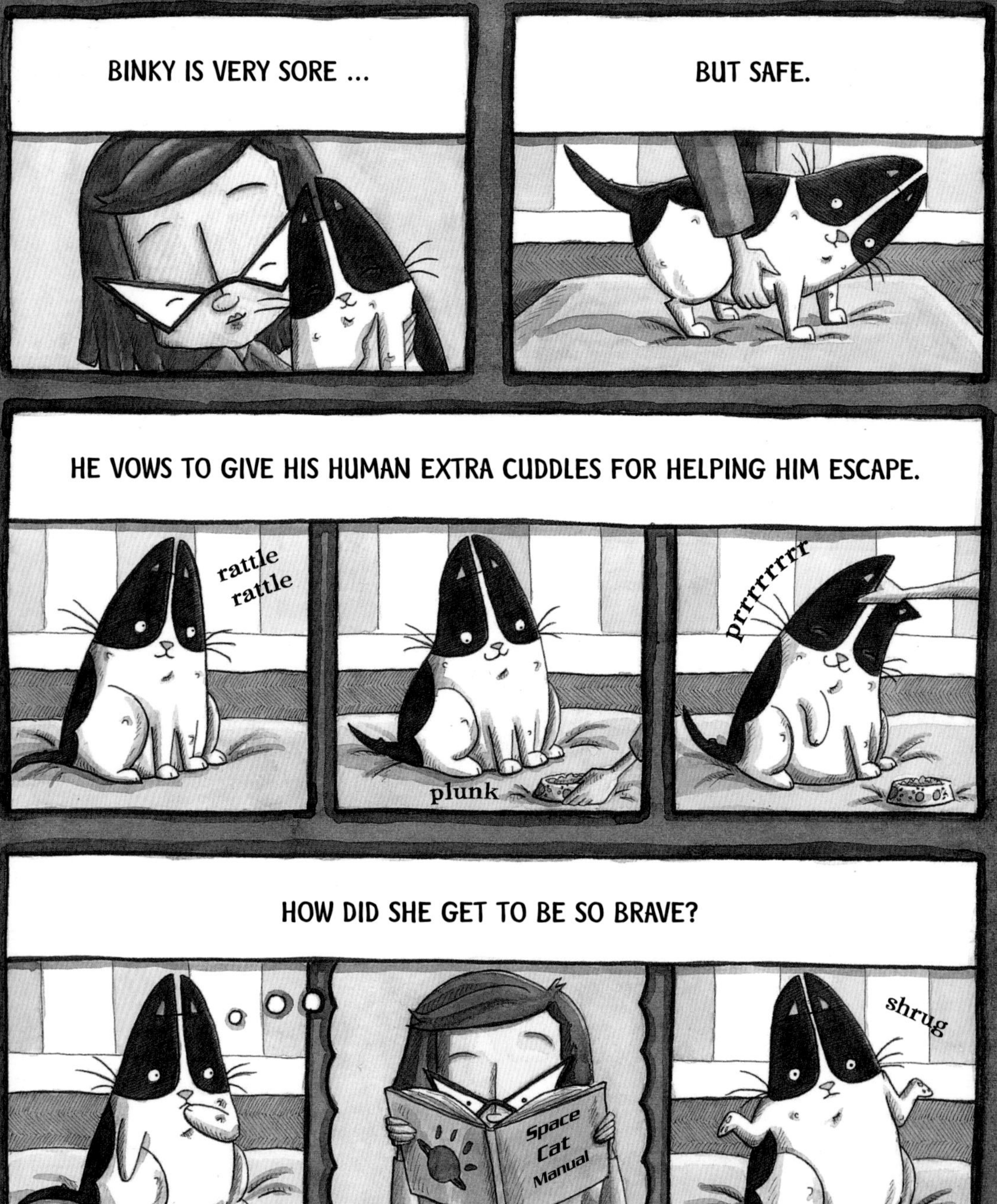
BINKY IS VERY SORE ...
BUT SAFE.
HE VOWS TO GIVE HIS HUMAN EXTRA CUDDLES FOR HELPING HIM ESCAPE.
rattle rattle
plunk
prrrrrrrr
HOW DID SHE GET TO BE SO BRAVE?
Space Cat Manual
shrug
HE HOPES SHE HASN'T BEEN READING HIS F.U.R.S.T. MANUALS WHEN HE ISN'T AROUND.

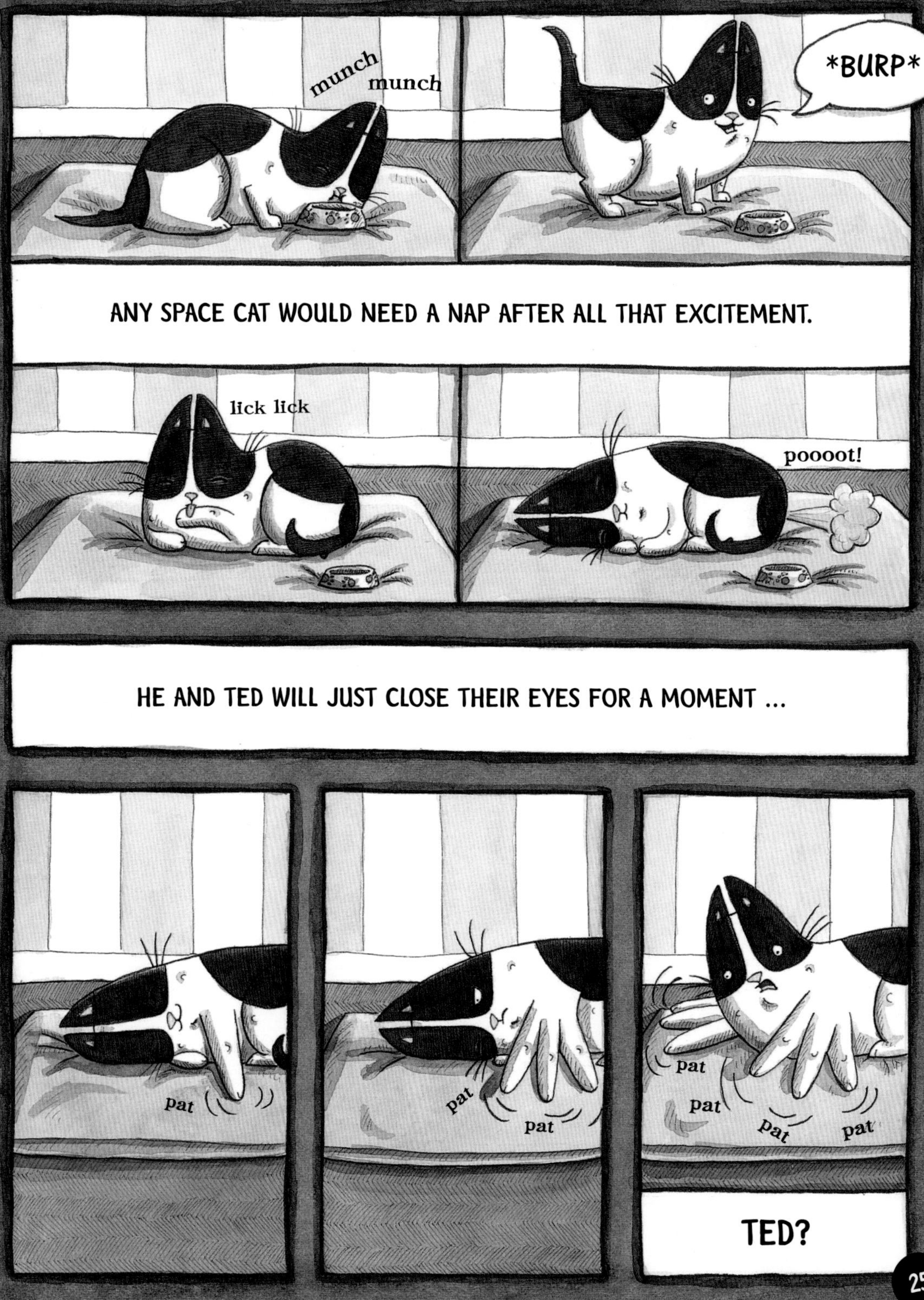
munch munch
BURP
ANY SPACE CAT WOULD NEED A NAP AFTER ALL THAT EXCITEMENT.
lick lick
poooot!
HE AND TED WILL JUST CLOSE THEIR EYES FOR A MOMENT ...
pat
pat
pat
pat
pat
pat
pat
TED?

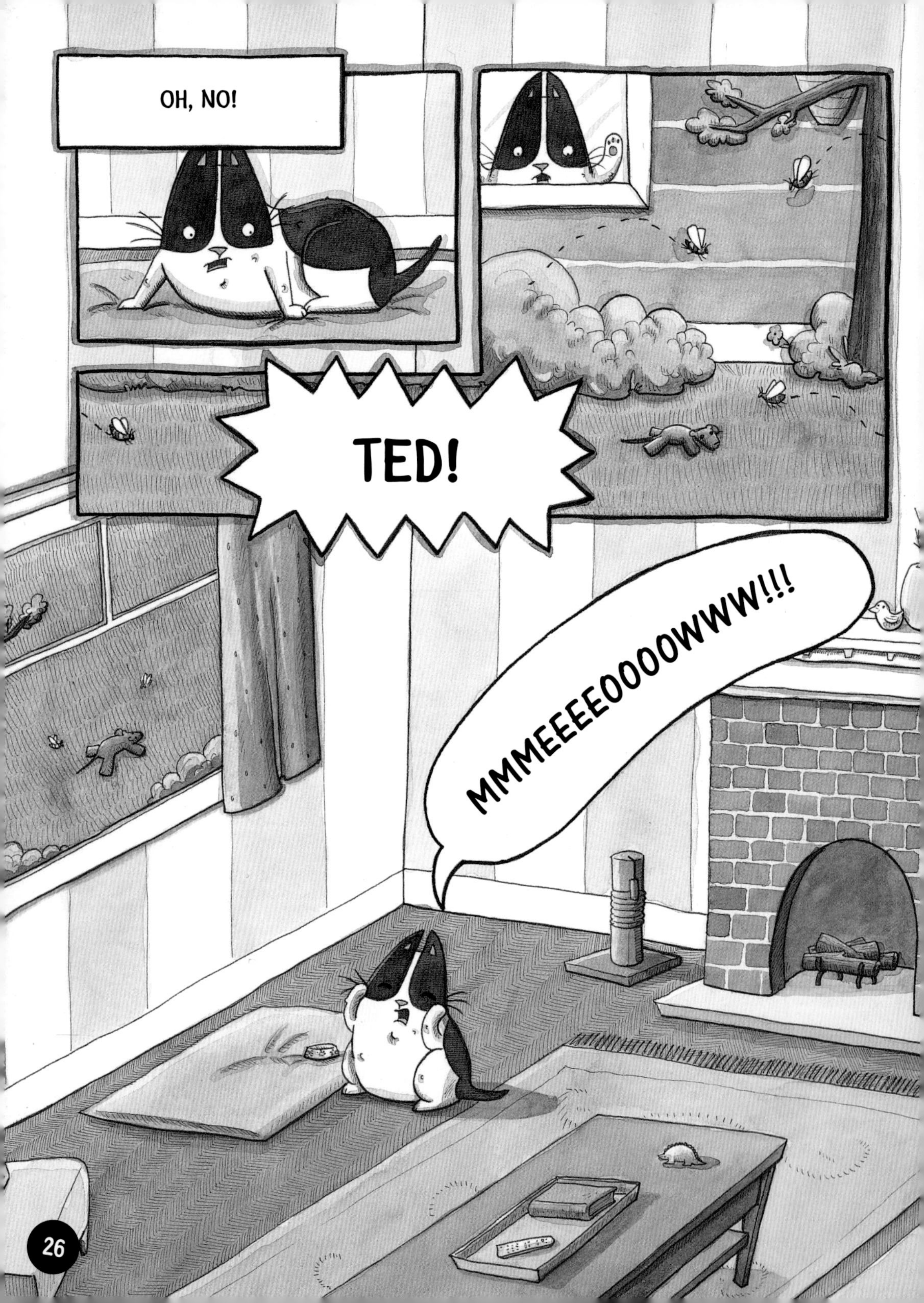
OH, NO!
TED!
MMMEEEEOOOOWWW!!!

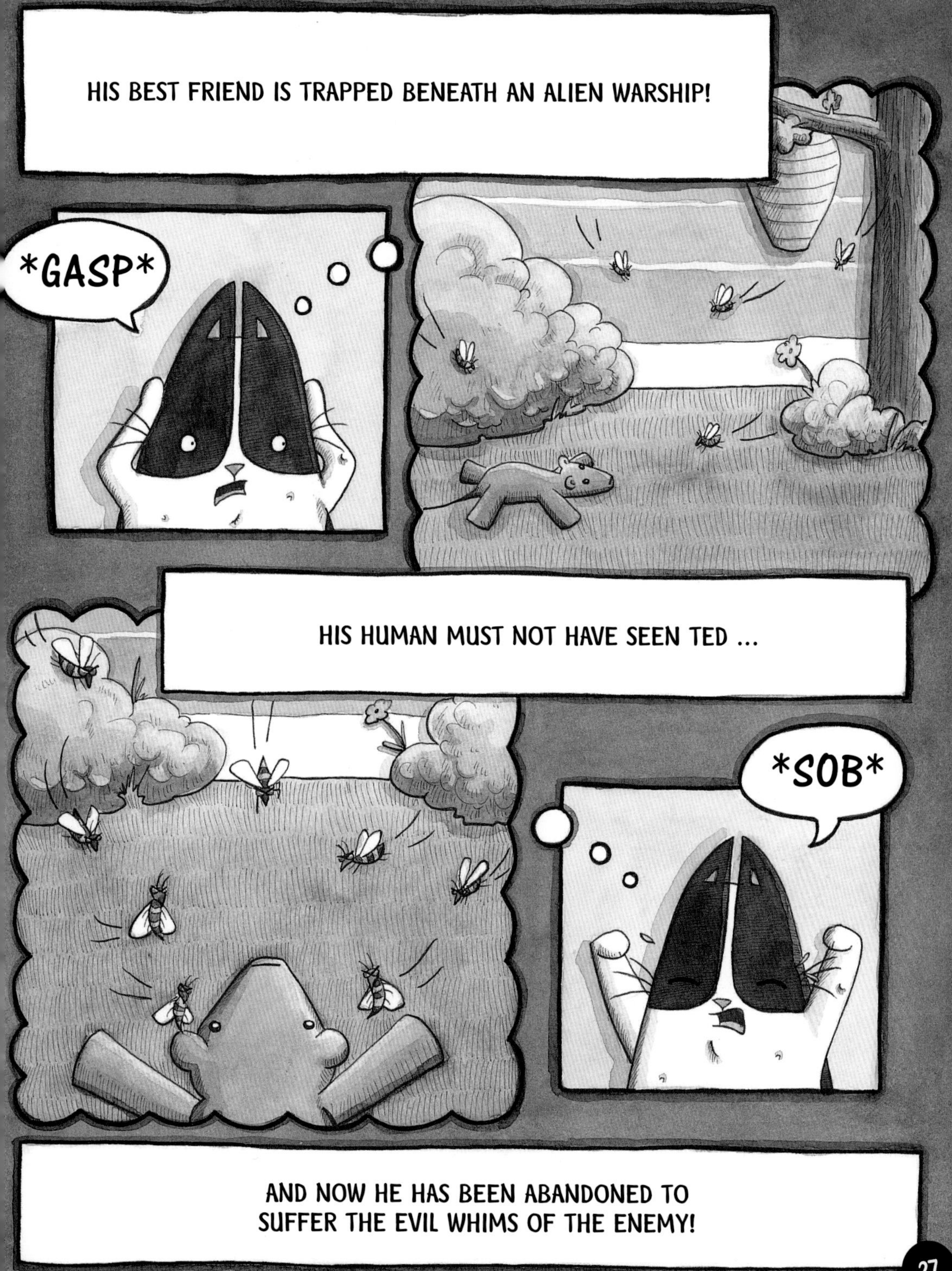
HIS BEST FRIEND IS TRAPPED BENEATH AN ALIEN WARSHIP!
GASP
HIS HUMAN MUST NOT HAVE SEEN TED ...
SOB
AND NOW HE HAS BEEN ABANDONED TO SUFFER THE EVIL WHIMS OF THE ENEMY!

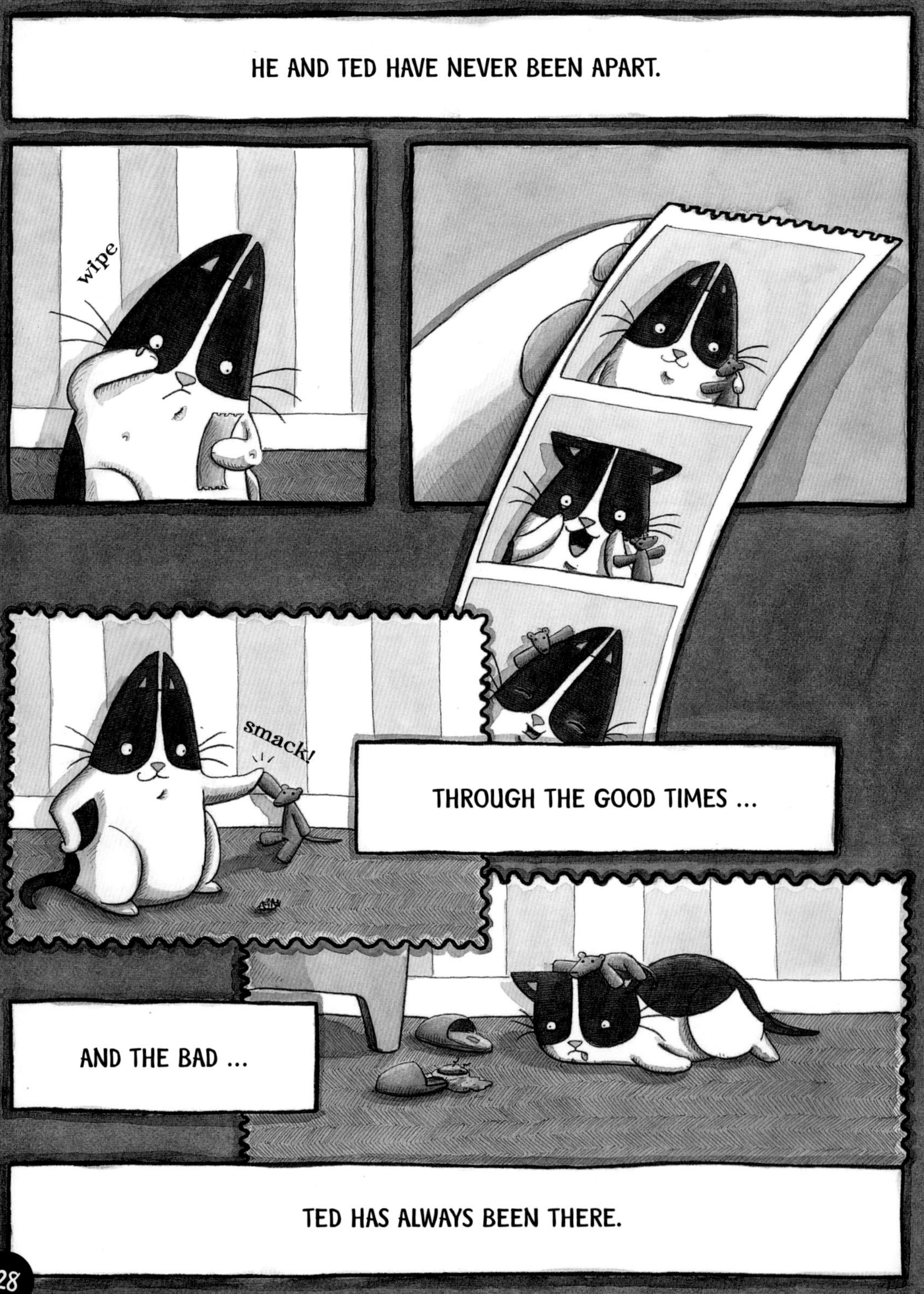

HE AND TED HAVE NEVER BEEN APART.
wipe
THROUGH THE GOOD TIMES ...
smack!
AND THE BAD ...
TED HAS ALWAYS BEEN THERE.

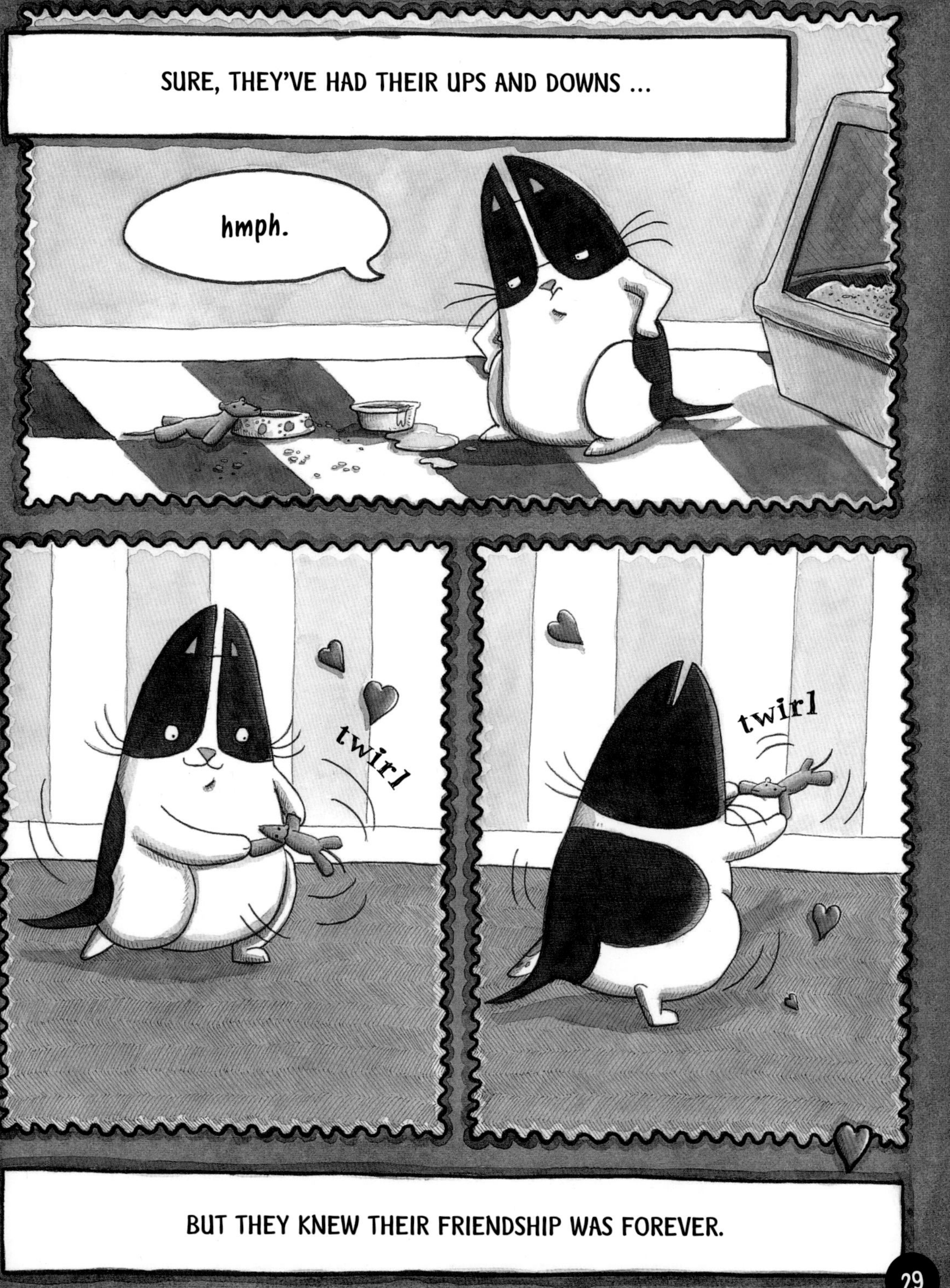
SURE, THEY'VE HAD THEIR UPS AND DOWNS ...
hmph.
twirl
twirl
BUT THEY KNEW THEIR FRIENDSHIP WAS FOREVER.

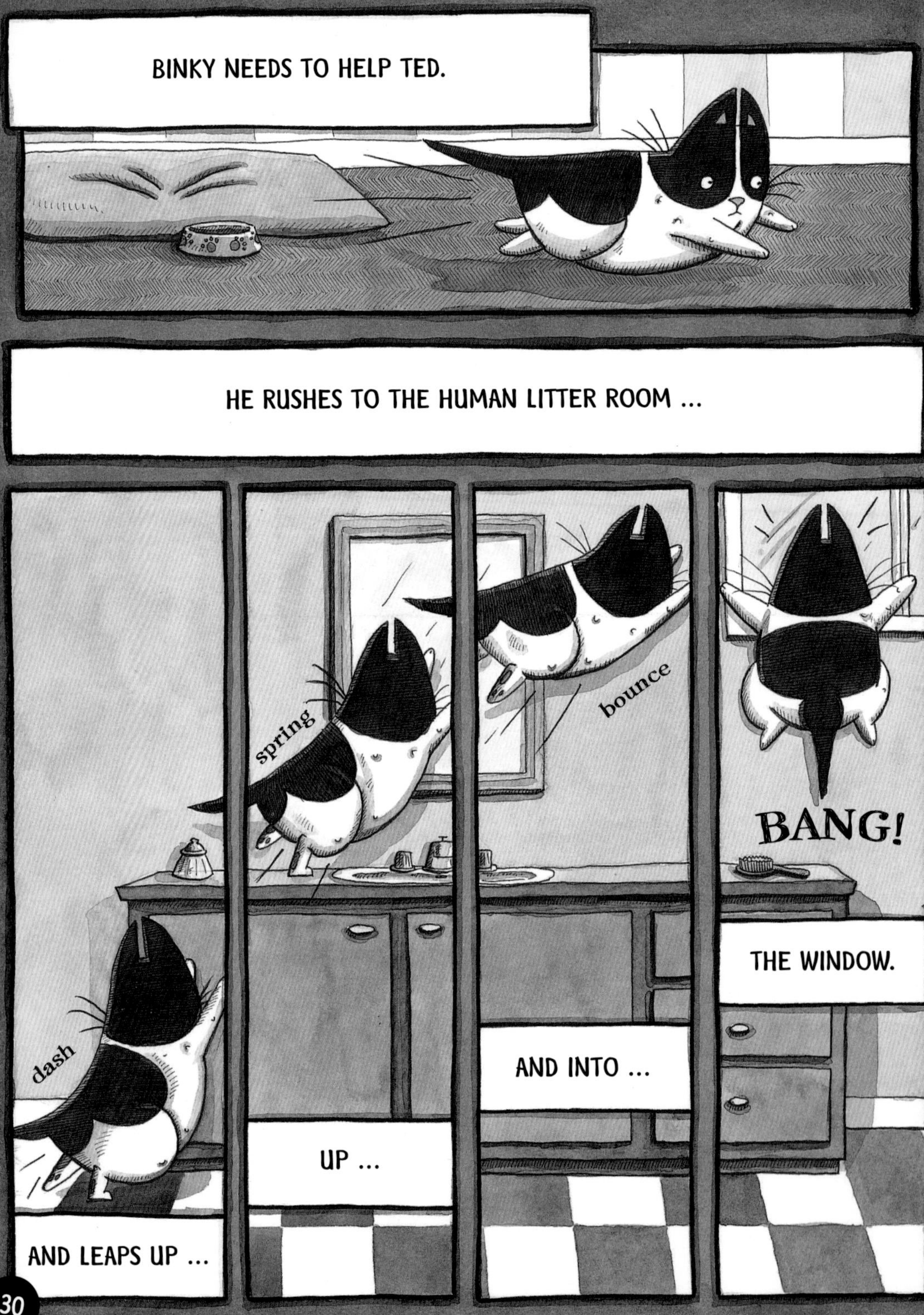

BINKY NEEDS TO HELP TED.
HE RUSHES TO THE HUMAN LITTER ROOM ...
dash
AND LEAPS UP ...
spring
UP ...
bounce
AND INTO ...
BANG!
THE WINDOW.

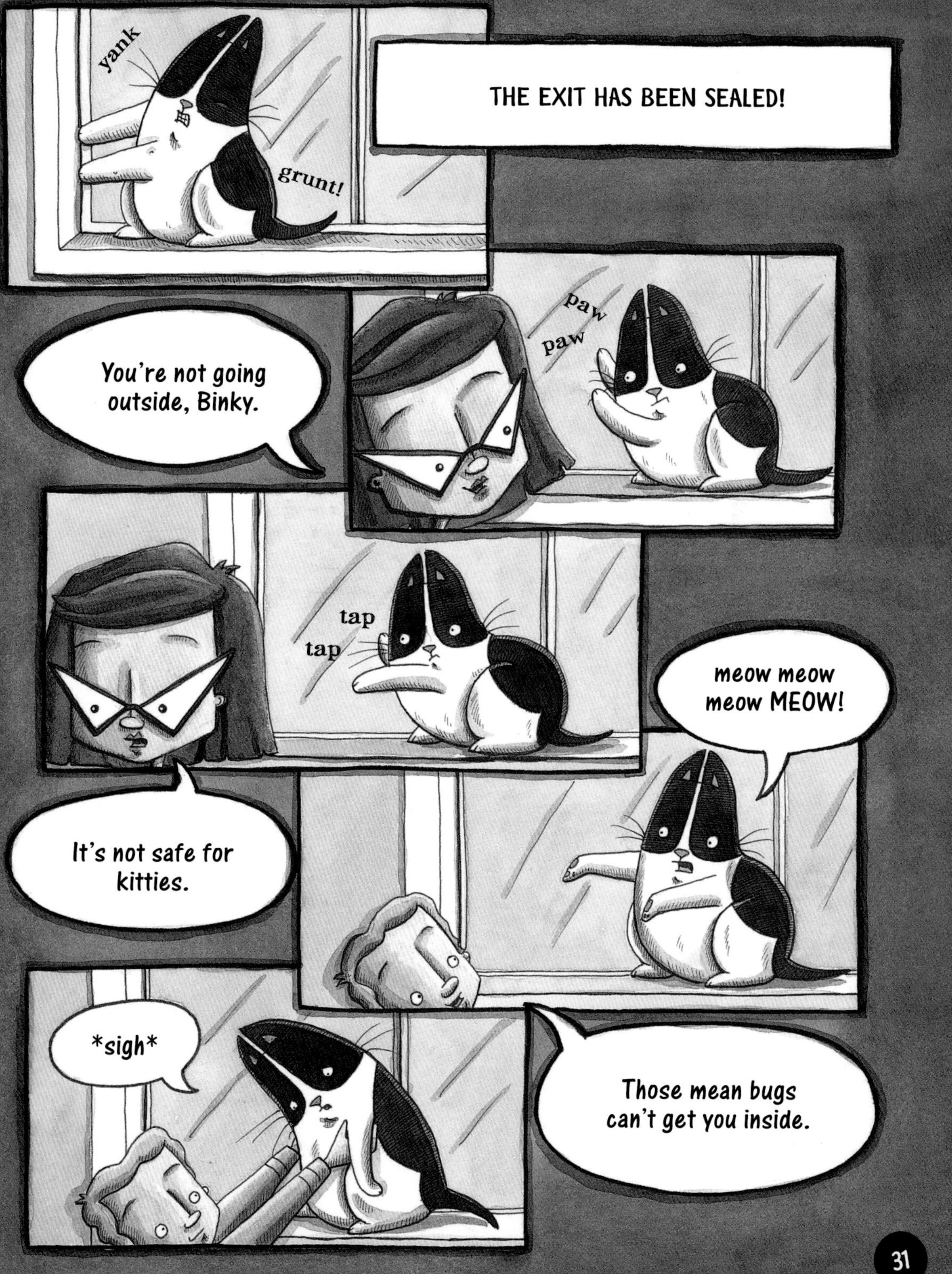

yank
grunt!
THE EXIT HAS BEEN SEALED!
paw
paw
You're not going outside, Binky.
tap
tap
meow meow meow MEOW!
It's not safe for kitties.
sigh
Those mean bugs can't get you inside.

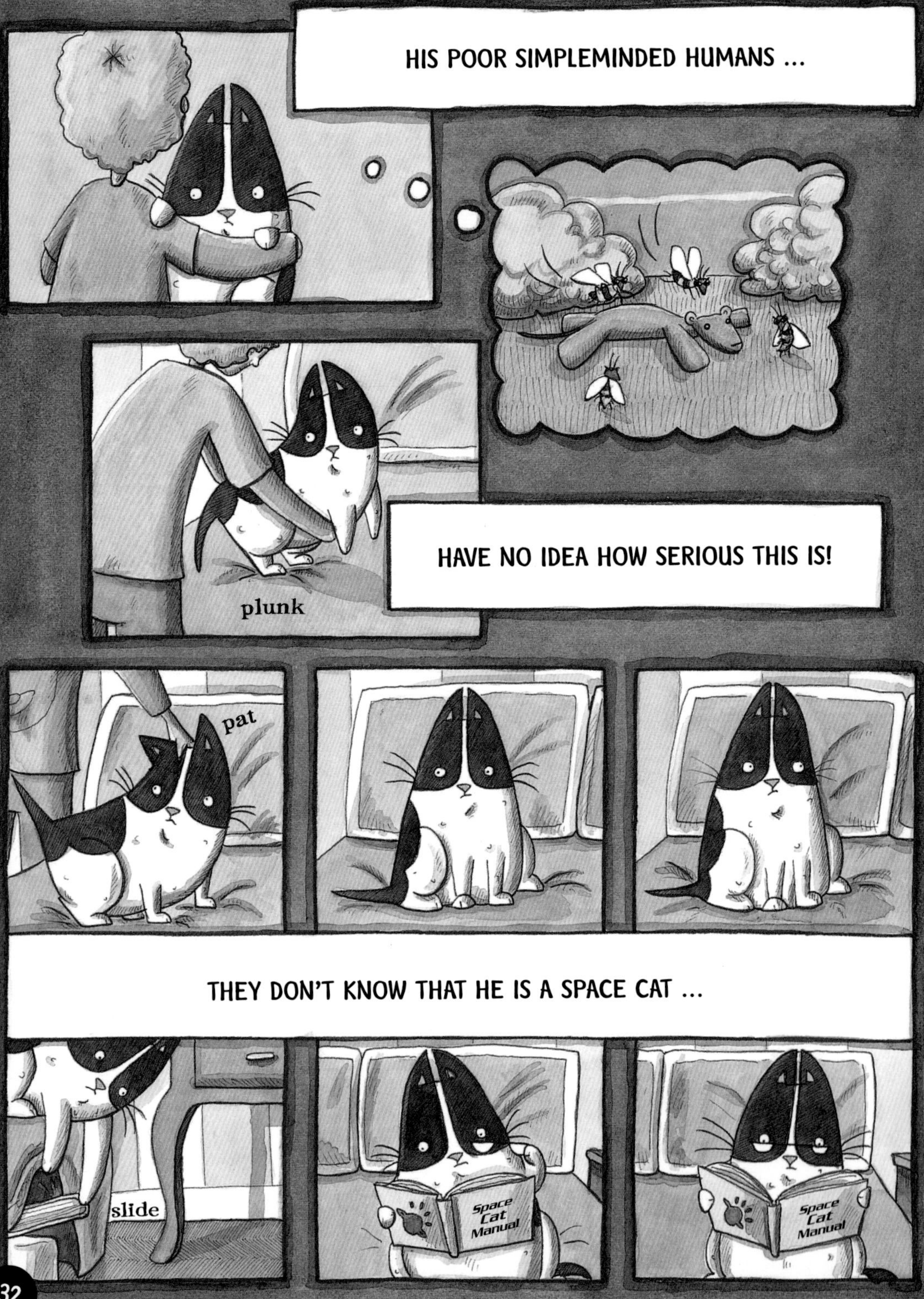
HIS POOR SIMPLEMINDED HUMANS ...
HAVE NO IDEA HOW SERIOUS THIS IS!
plunk
pat
THEY DON'T KNOW THAT HE IS A SPACE CAT ...
slide
Space Cat Manual
Space Cat Manual

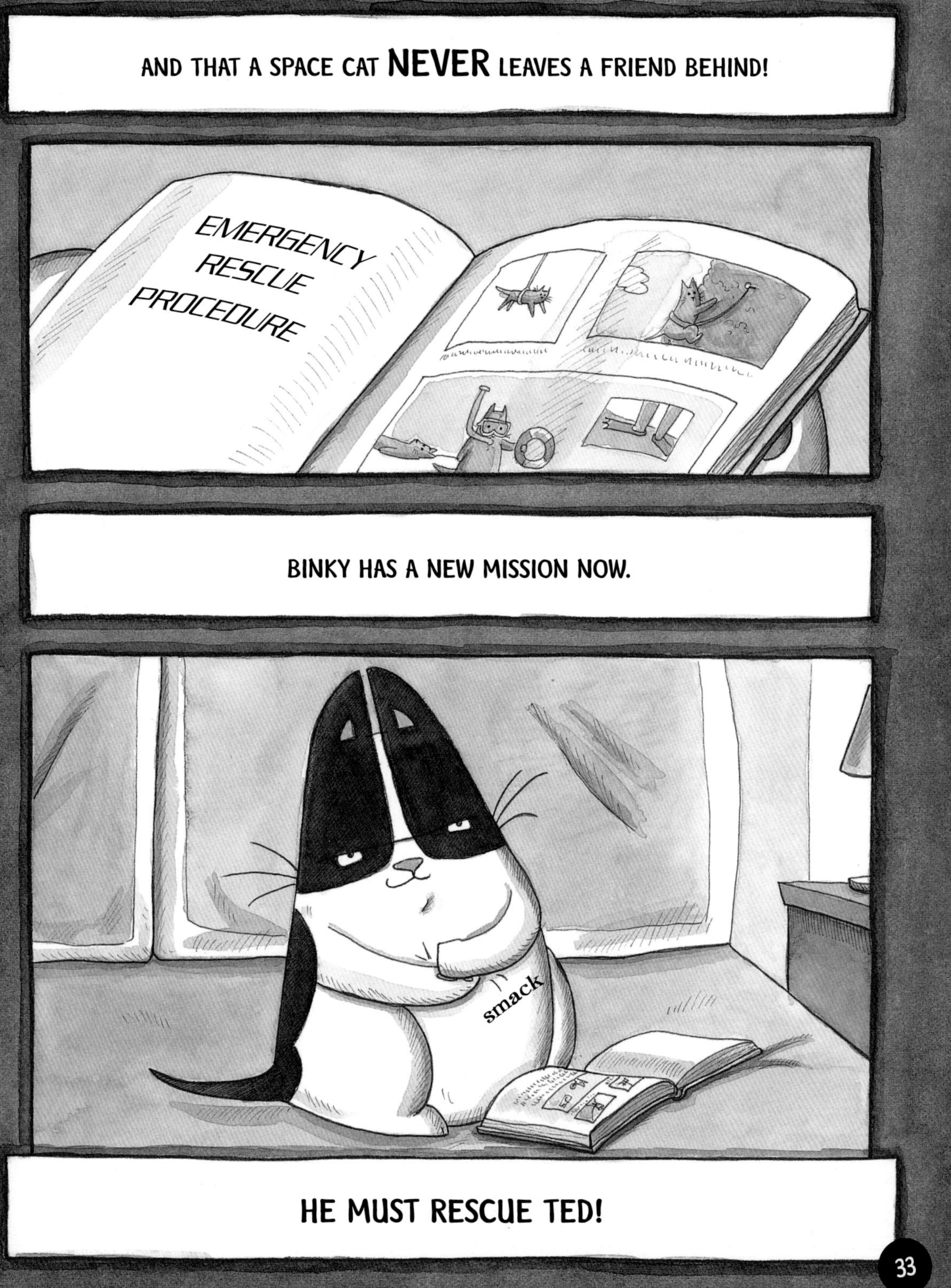
AND THAT A SPACE CAT NEVER LEAVES A FRIEND BEHIND!
EMERGENCY RESCUE PROCEDURE
BINKY HAS A NEW MISSION NOW.
smack
HE MUST RESCUE TED!

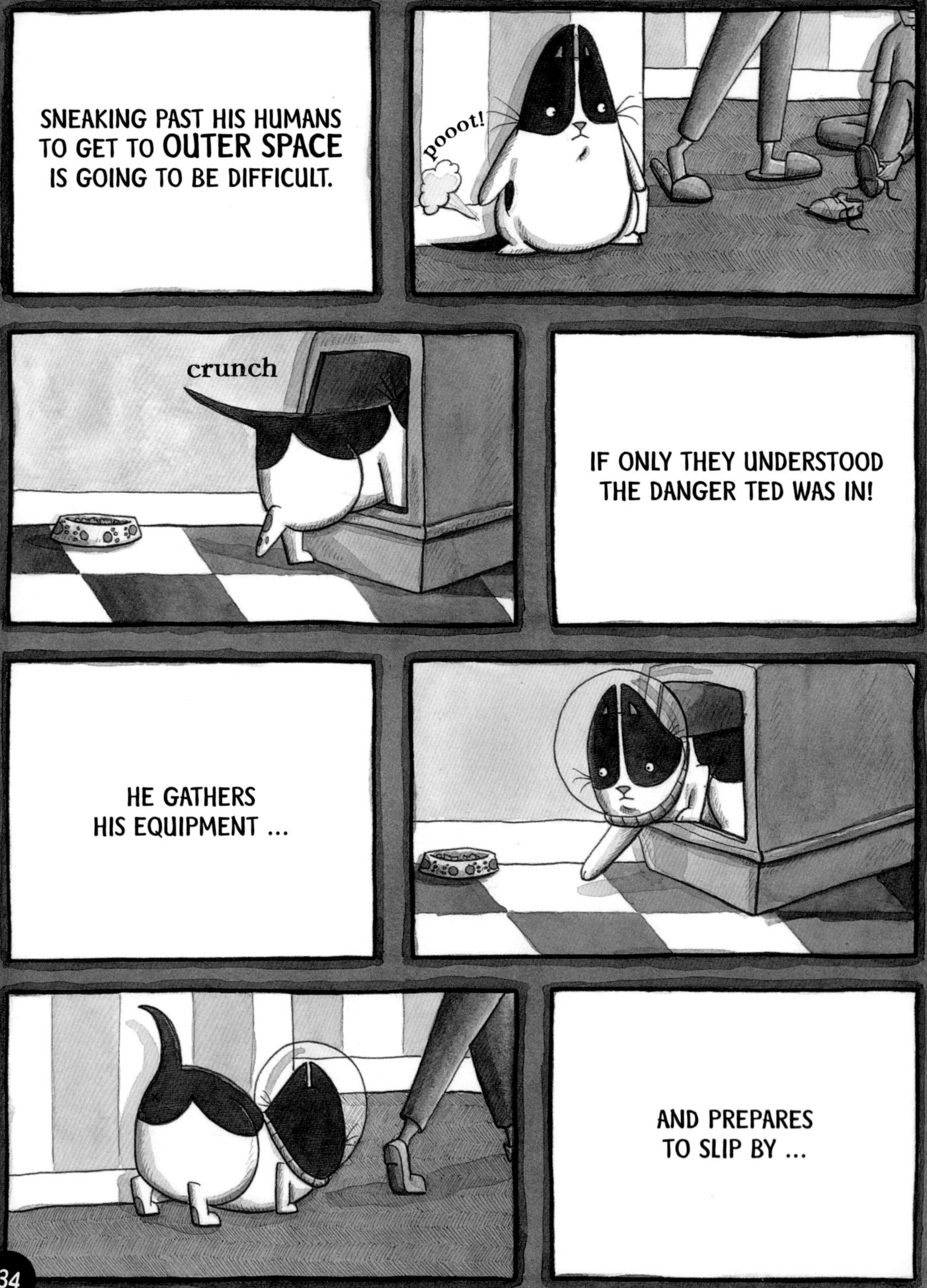
SNEAKING PAST HIS HUMANS TO GET TO OUTER SPACE IS GOING TO BE DIFFICULT.
pooot!
crunch
IF ONLY THEY UNDERSTOOD THE DANGER TED WAS IN!
HE GATHERS HIS EQUIPMENT ...
AND PREPARES TO SLIP BY ...

woooooosh

BOOF!

BUT THEY MANAGE TO THWART HIS EVERY ATTEMPT.

No way, Binkster!

SUDDENLY, IT OCCURS TO BINKY ...

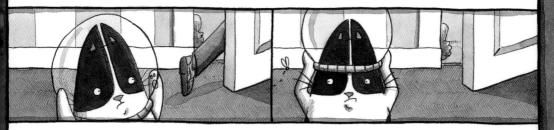

IF HE WANTS TO SAVE TED FROM THE ALIENS ...

bzzzzzz

SLAM!

HE HAS TO **THINK** LIKE AN ALIEN!

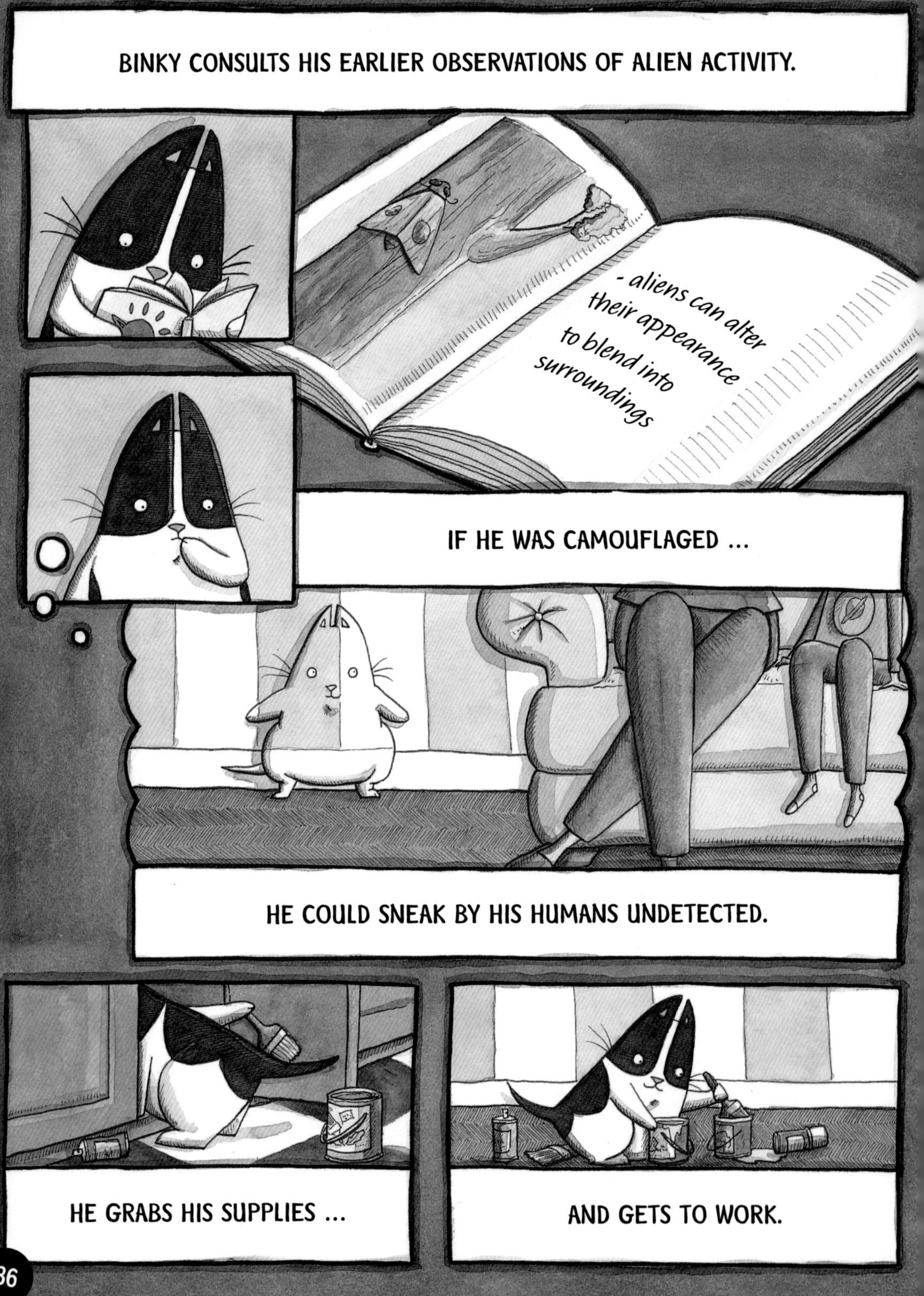
BINKY CONSULTS HIS EARLIER OBSERVATIONS OF ALIEN ACTIVITY.
- aliens can alter their appearance to blend into surroundings
IF HE WAS CAMOUFLAGED ...
HE COULD SNEAK BY HIS HUMANS UNDETECTED.
HE GRABS HIS SUPPLIES ...
AND GETS TO WORK.

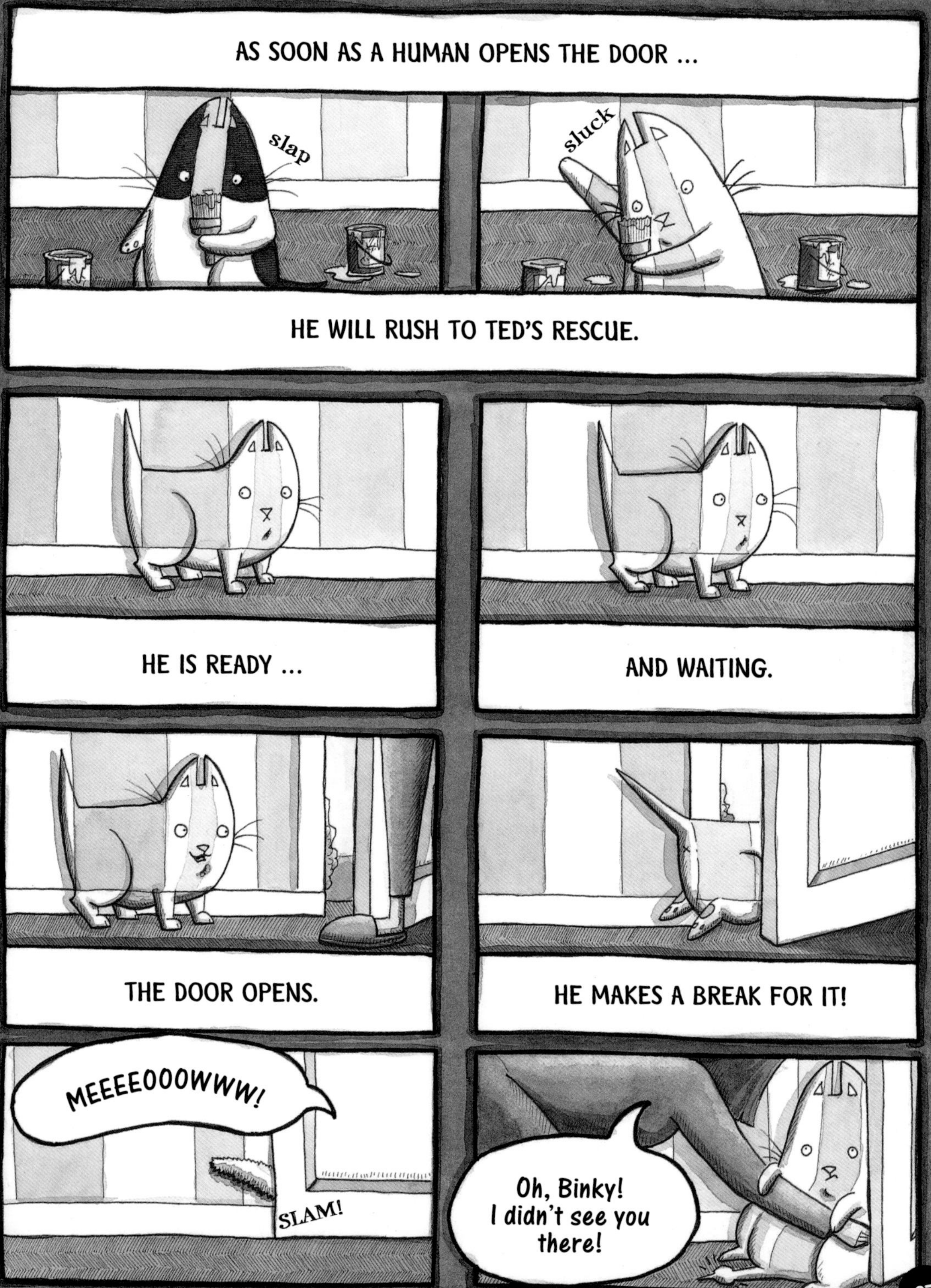
AS SOON AS A HUMAN OPENS THE DOOR ...
slap
sluck
HE WILL RUSH TO TED'S RESCUE.
HE IS READY ...
AND WAITING.
THE DOOR OPENS.
HE MAKES A BREAK FOR IT!
MEEEEOOOWWW!
SLAM!
Oh, Binky! I didn't see you there!

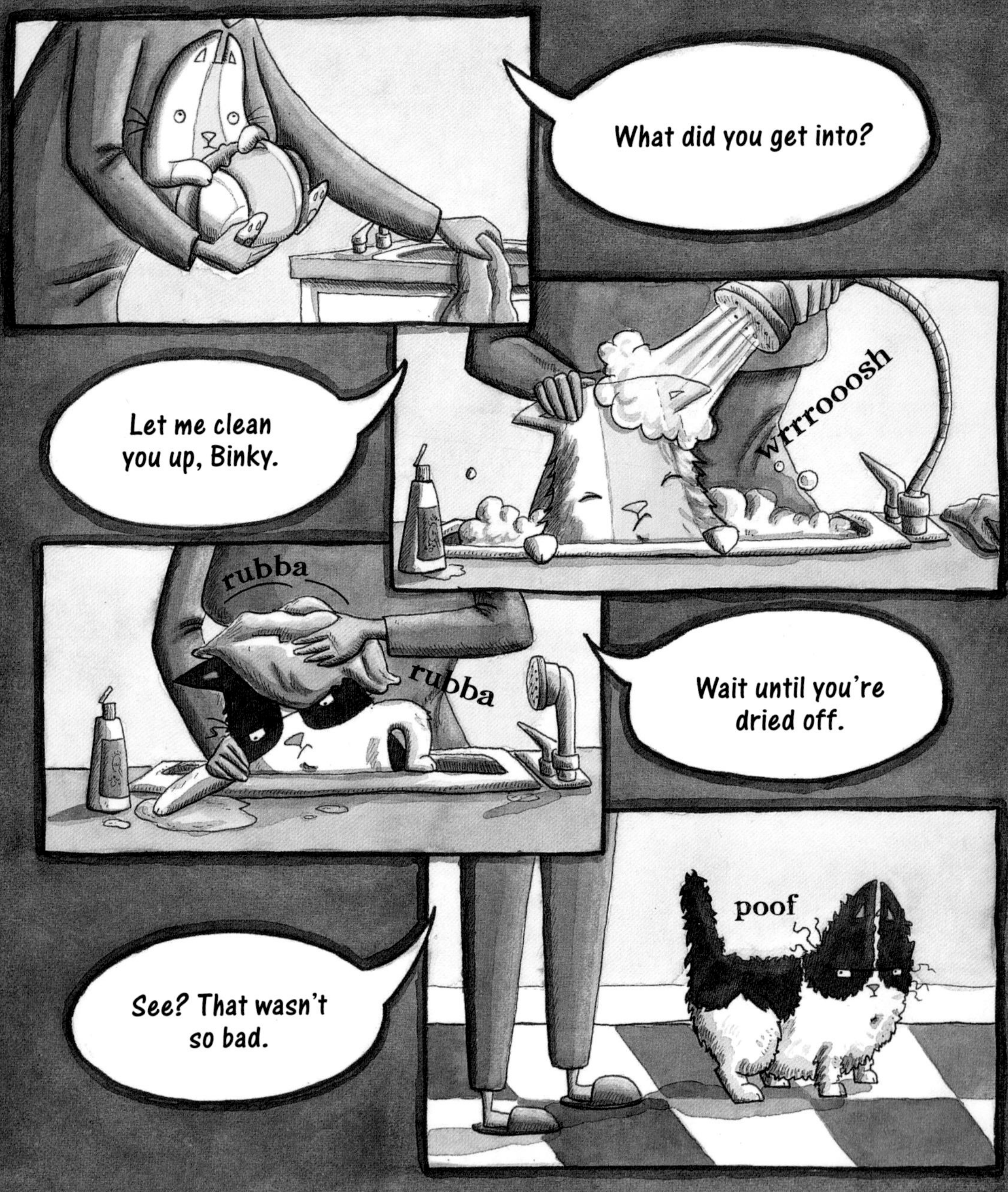
What did you get into?
Let me clean you up, Binky.
wrrrooosh
rubba
rubba
Wait until you're dried off.
poof
See? That wasn't so bad.

MAYBE HE WOULD BE BETTER OFF WITH A DIFFERENT PLAN OF ACTION.

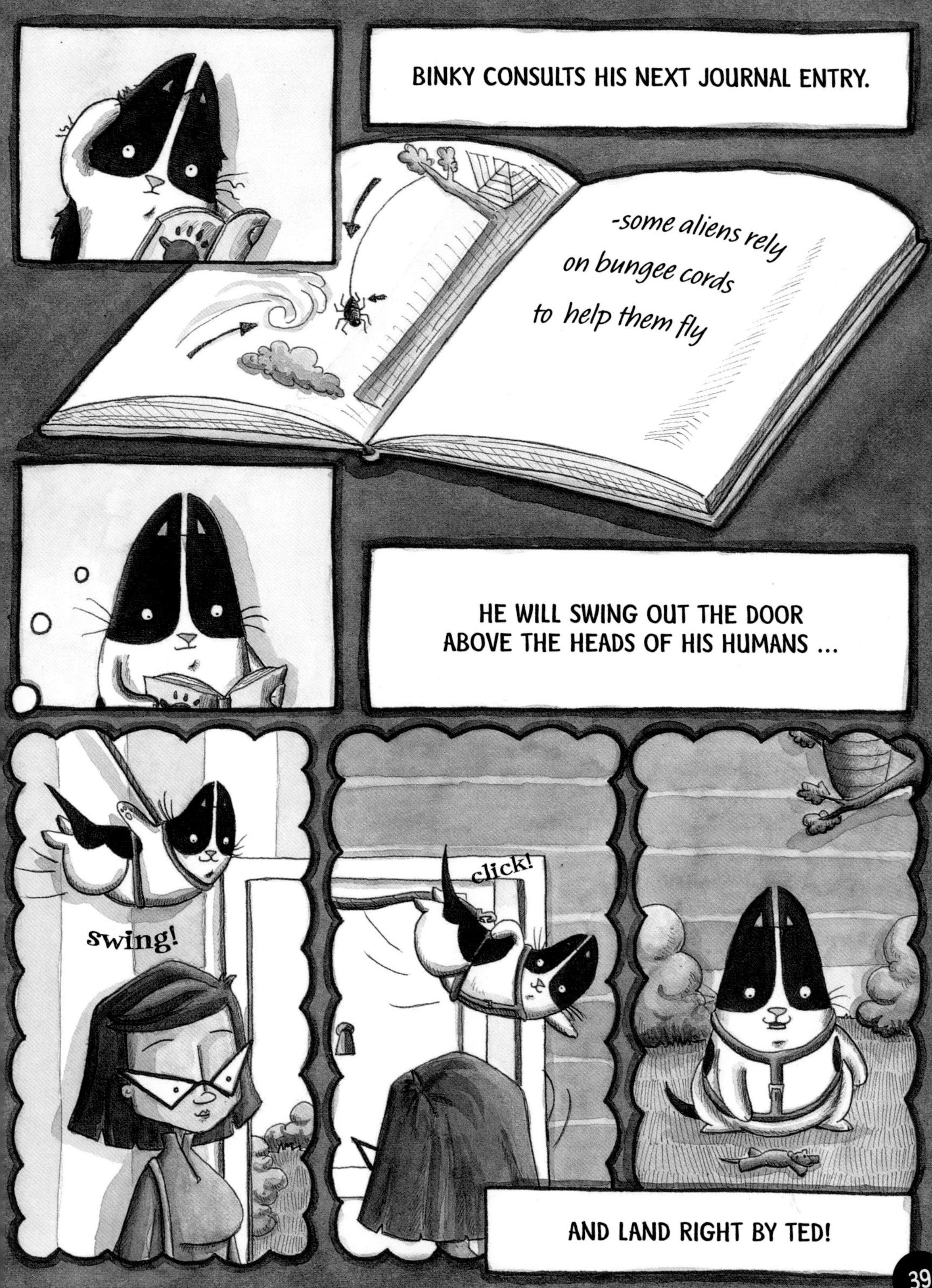

BINKY CONSULTS HIS NEXT JOURNAL ENTRY.
-some aliens rely on bungee cords to help them fly
HE WILL SWING OUT THE DOOR ABOVE THE HEADS OF HIS HUMANS ...
swing!
click!
AND LAND RIGHT BY TED!

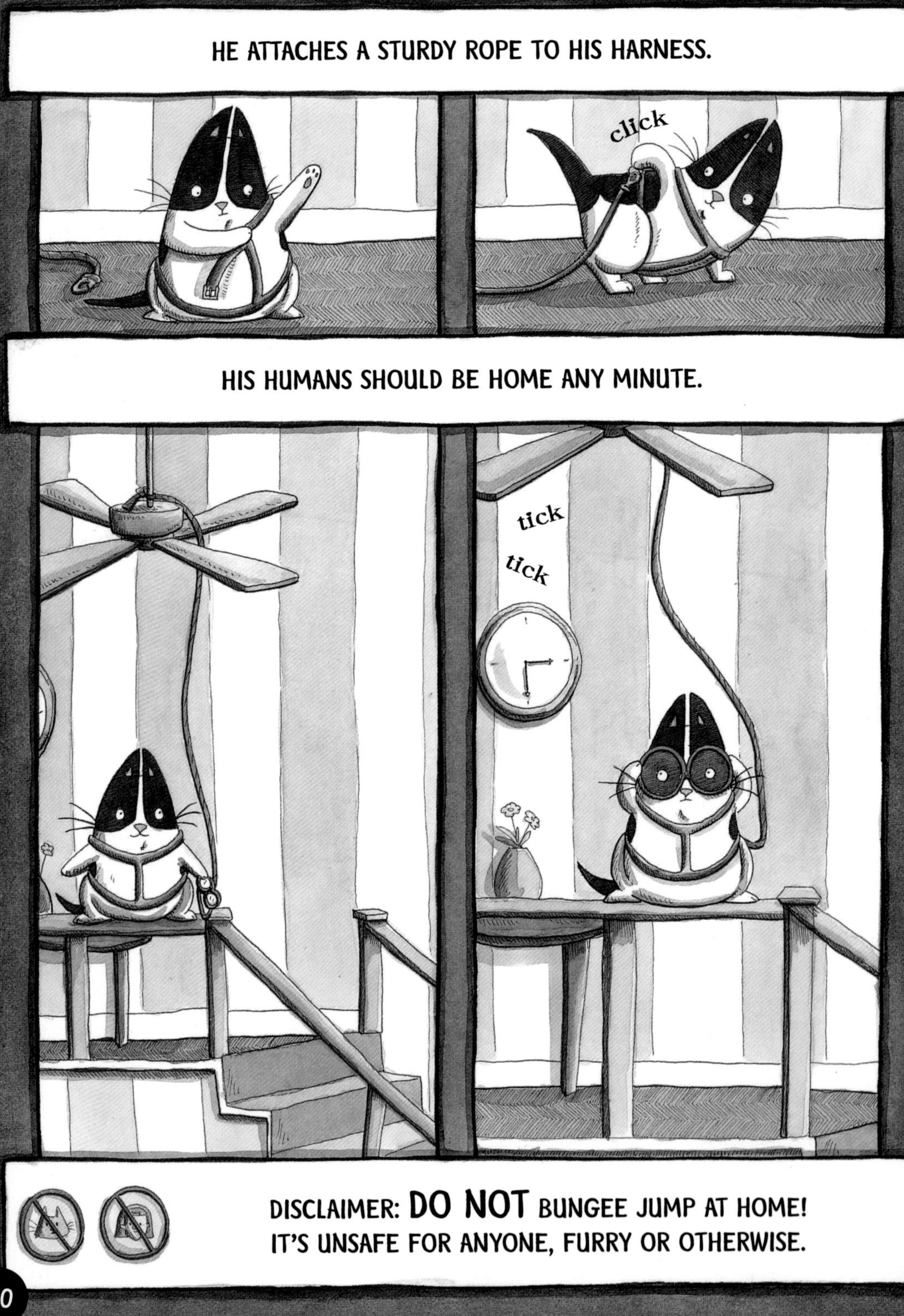
HE ATTACHES A STURDY ROPE TO HIS HARNESS.
click
HIS HUMANS SHOULD BE HOME ANY MINUTE.
tick
tick
DISCLAIMER: DO NOT BUNGEE JUMP AT HOME!
IT'S UNSAFE FOR ANYONE, FURRY OR OTHERWISE.

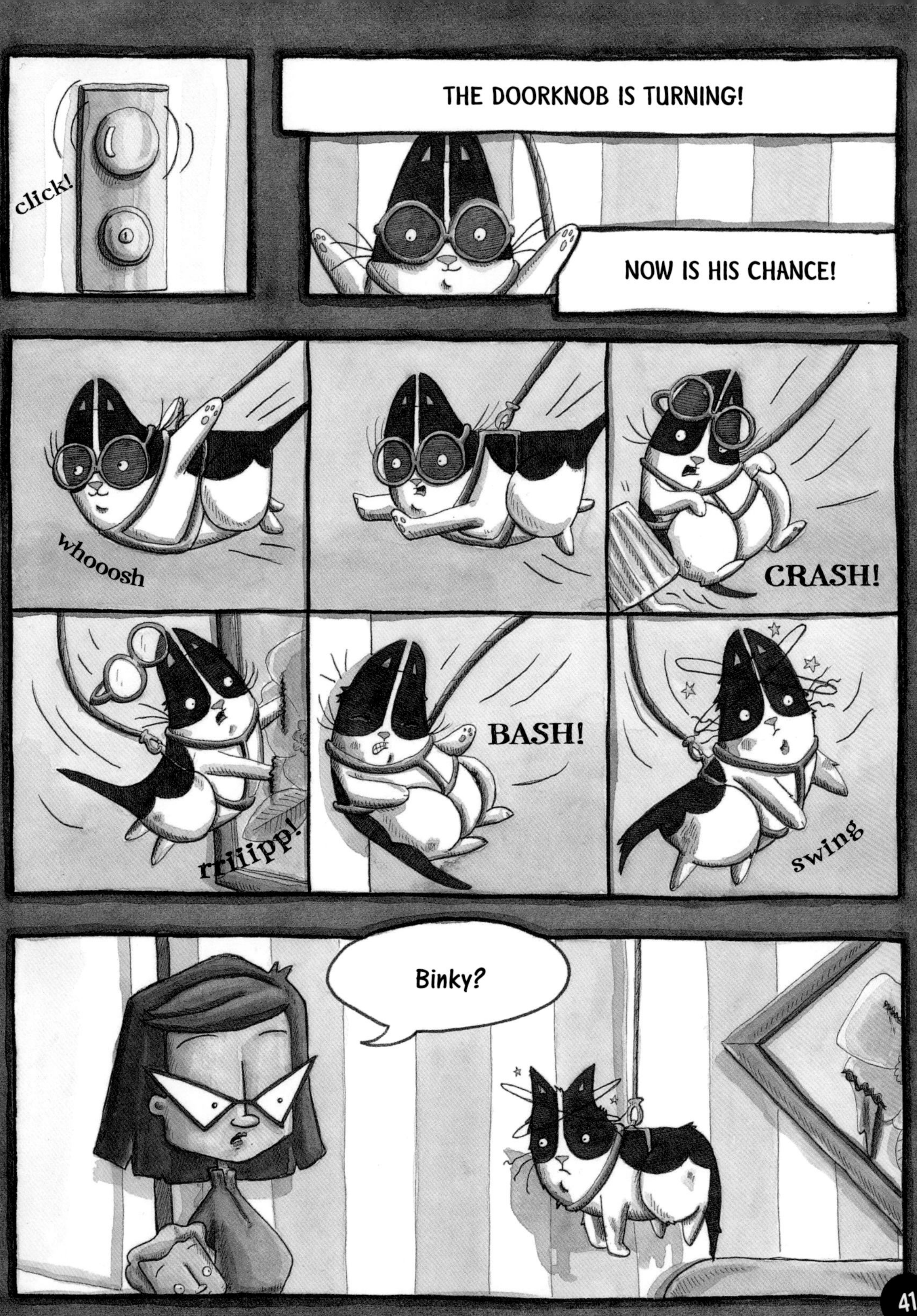
click!
THE DOORKNOB IS TURNING!
NOW IS HIS CHANCE!
whooosh
CRASH!
rriiipp!
BASH!
swing
Binky?

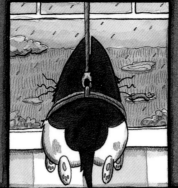

HE JUST CAN'T LEAVE TED OUT THERE, ALL ALONE.

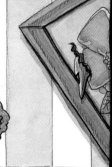

BUT TRYING TO GET OUT THE FRONT DOOR CLEARLY ISN'T WORKING.

Binky, try to behave!

42

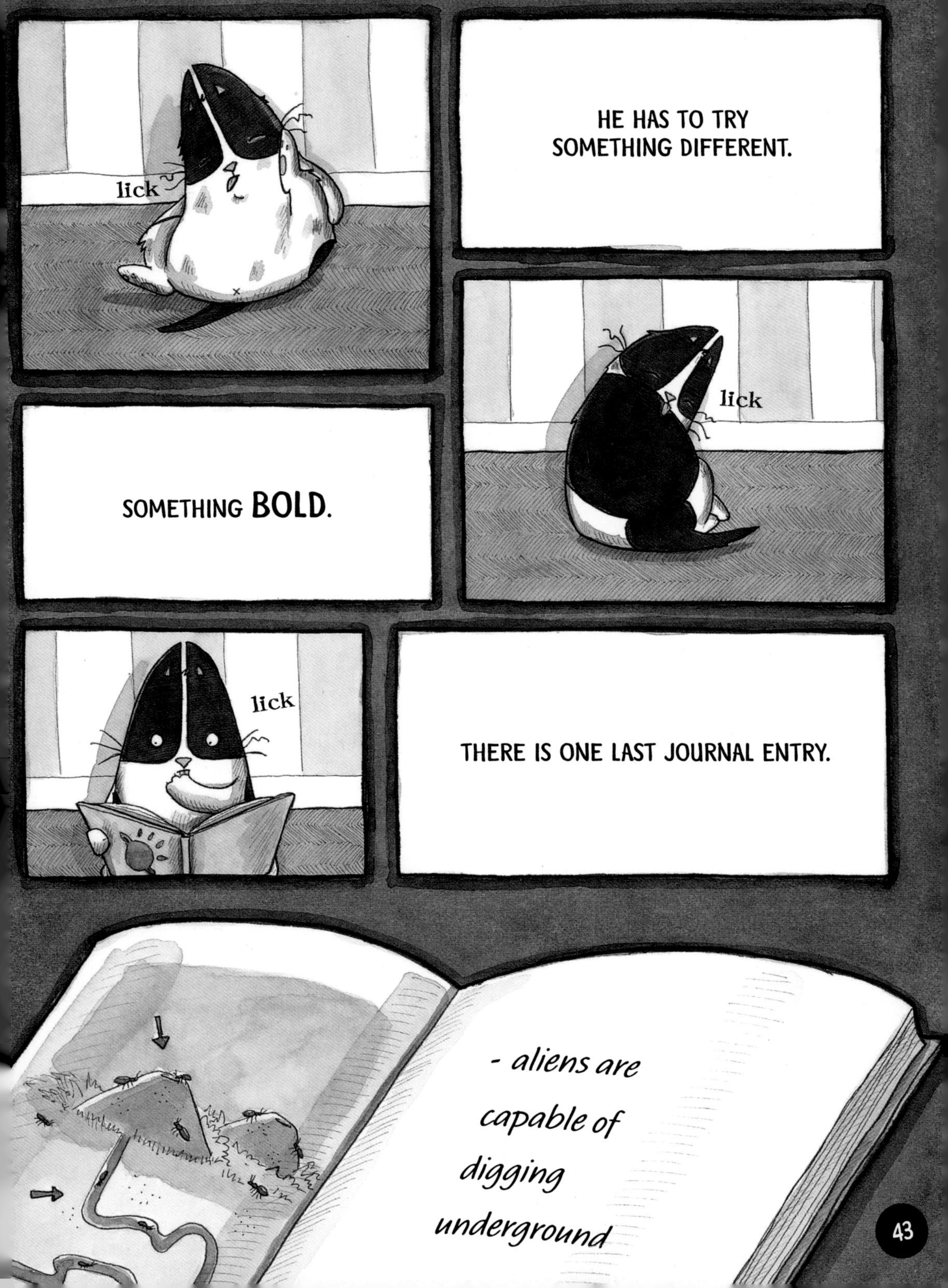
lick
HE HAS TO TRY SOMETHING DIFFERENT.
lick
SOMETHING BOLD.
lick
THERE IS ONE LAST JOURNAL ENTRY.
- aliens are capable of digging underground

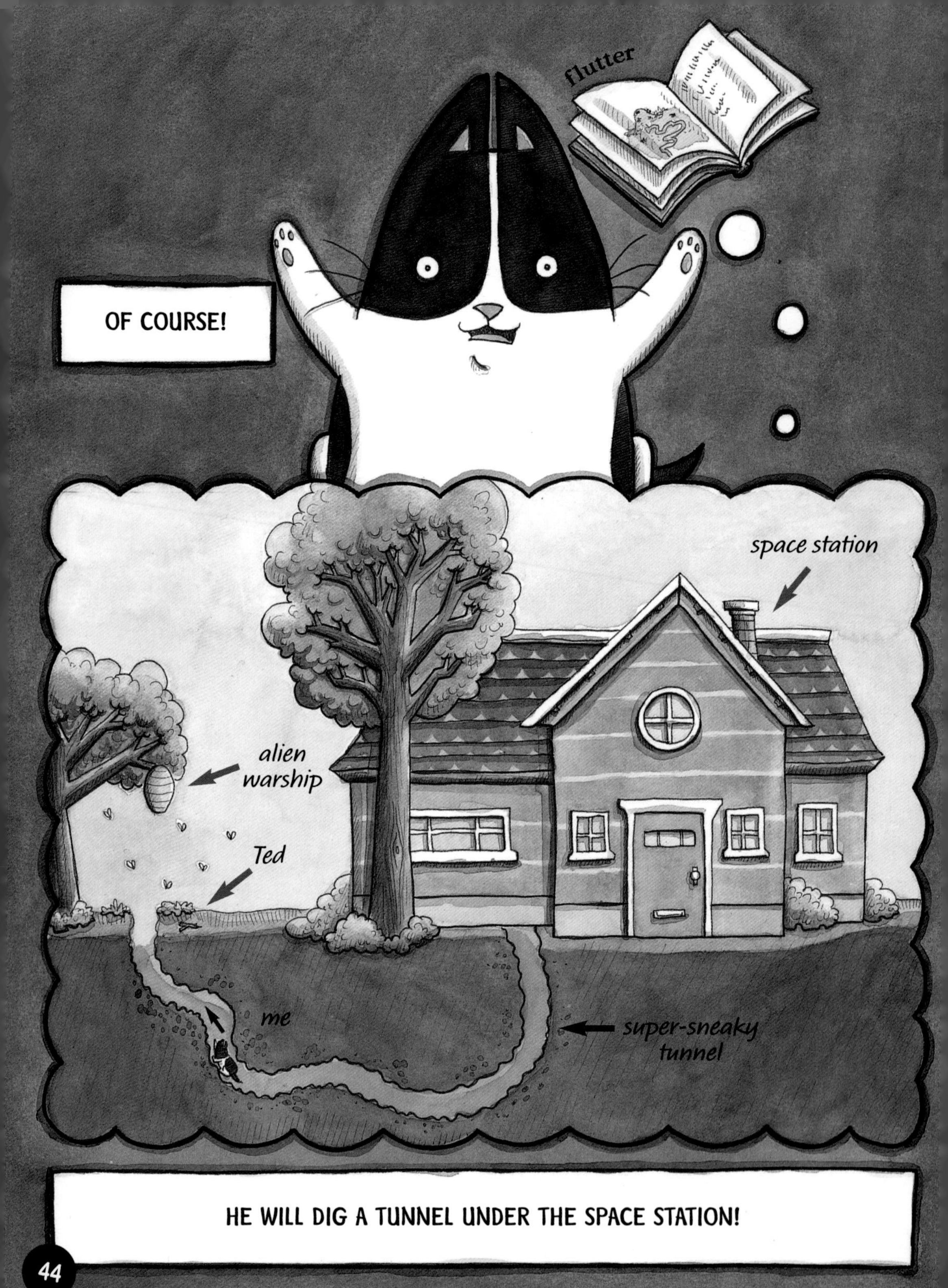

OF COURSE!
flutter
space station
alien
warship
Ted
me
super-sneaky
tunnel
HE WILL DIG A TUNNEL UNDER THE SPACE STATION!

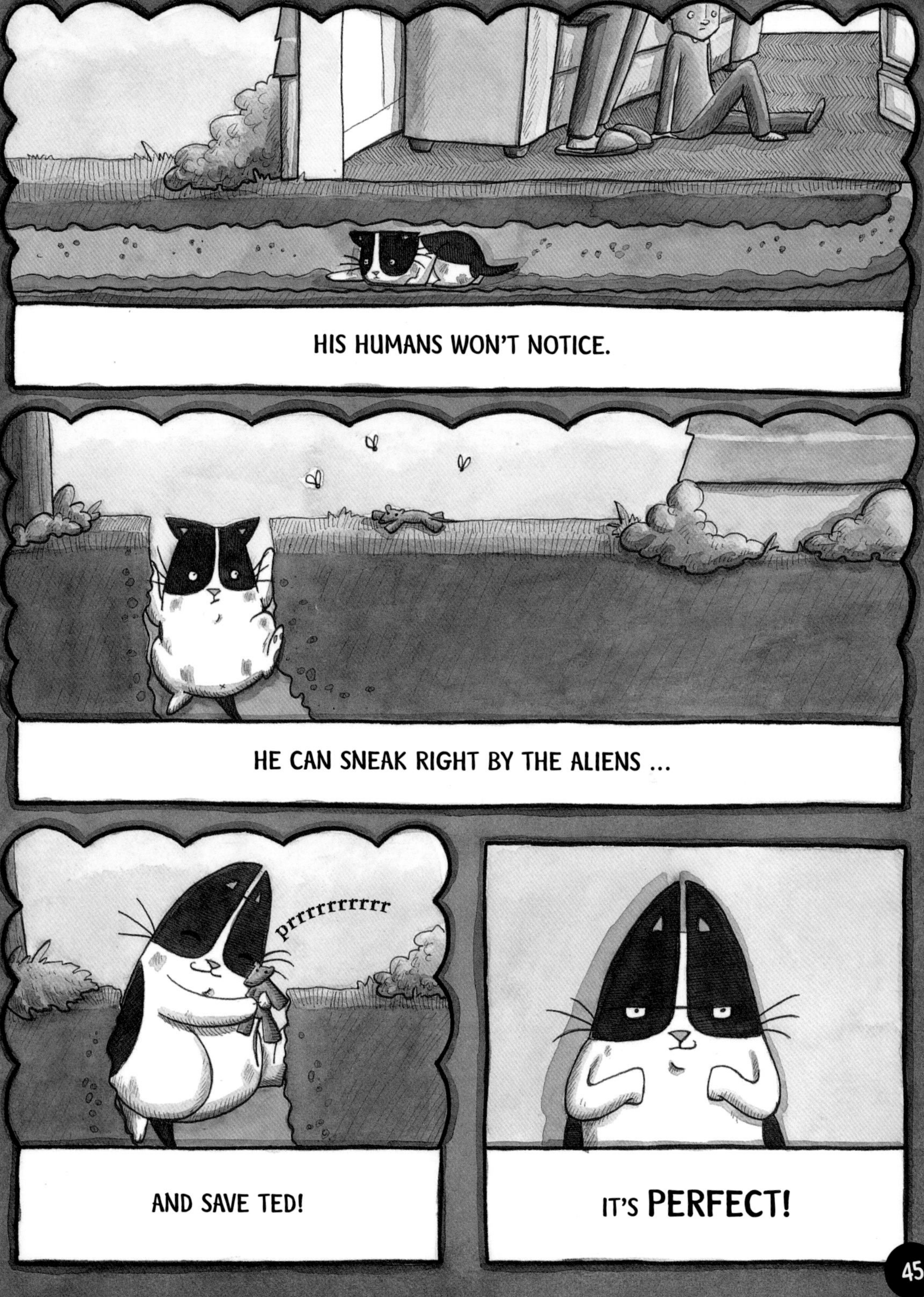
HIS HUMANS WON'T NOTICE.
HE CAN SNEAK RIGHT BY THE ALIENS ...
prrrrrrrrrr
AND SAVE TED!
IT'S PERFECT!

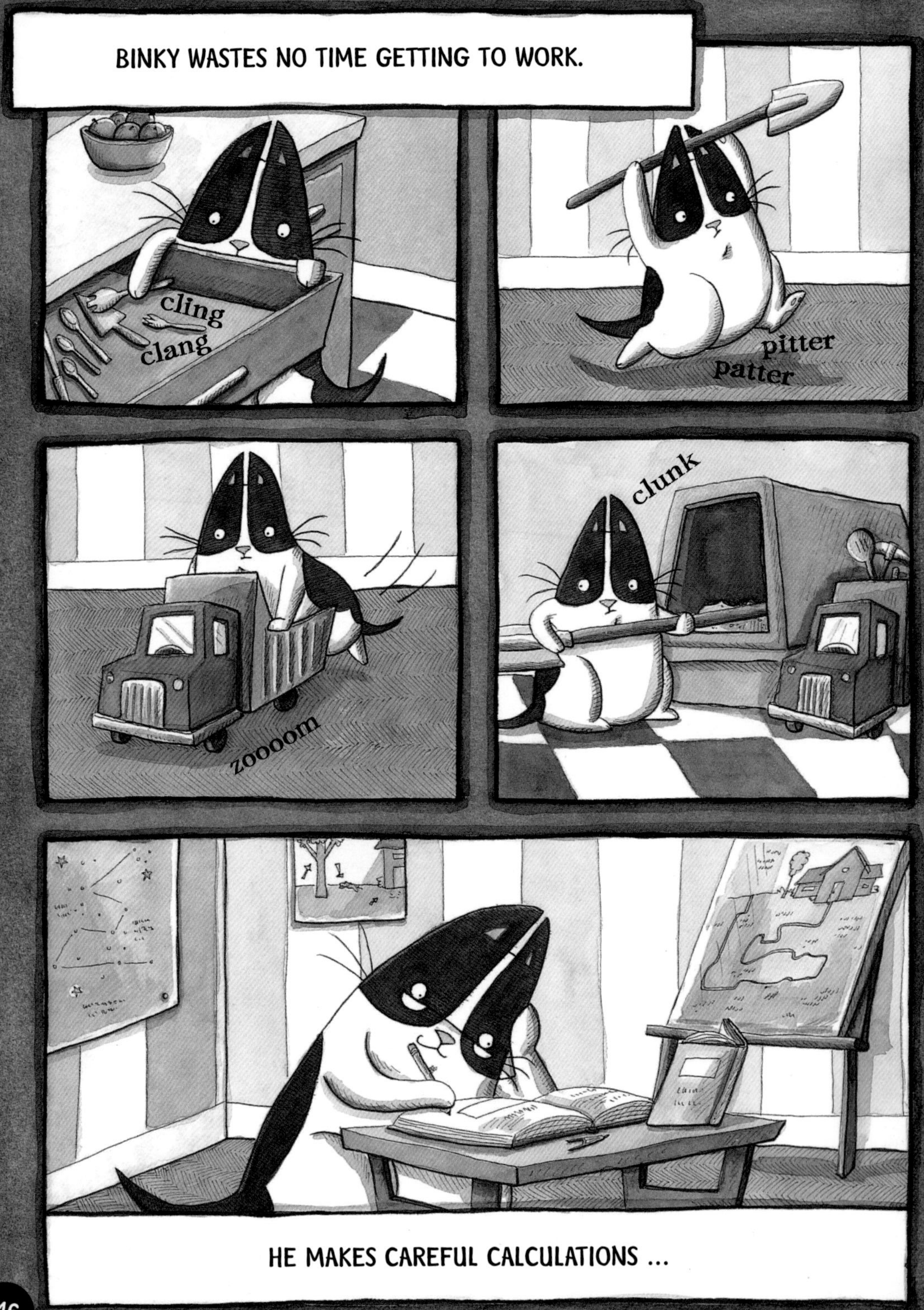
BINKY WASTES NO TIME GETTING TO WORK.
cling
clang
pitter
patter
zoooom
clunk
HE MAKES CAREFUL CALCULATIONS ...

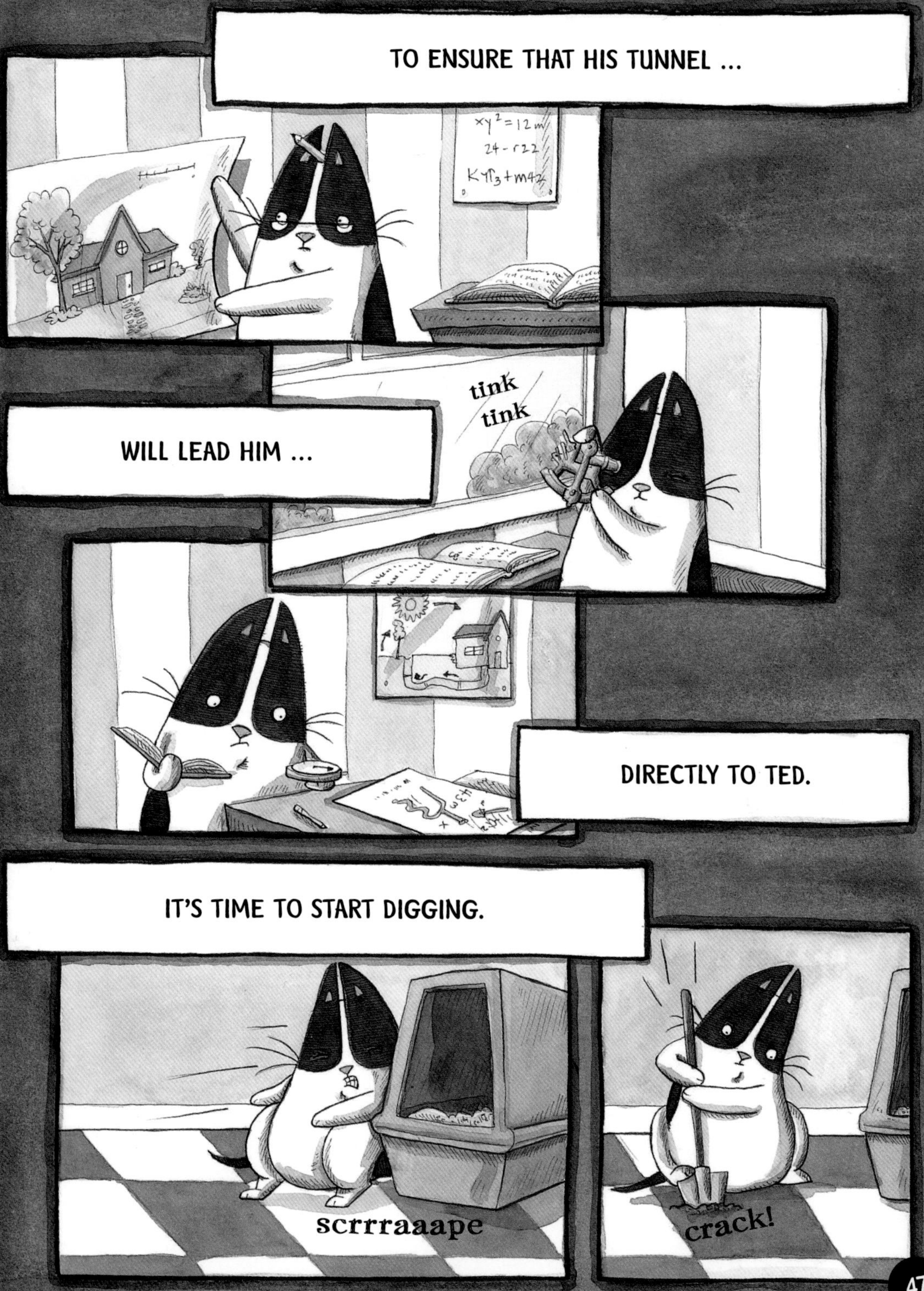
TO ENSURE THAT HIS TUNNEL ...
tink
tink
WILL LEAD HIM ...
DIRECTLY TO TED.
IT'S TIME TO START DIGGING.
scrrraaape
crack!

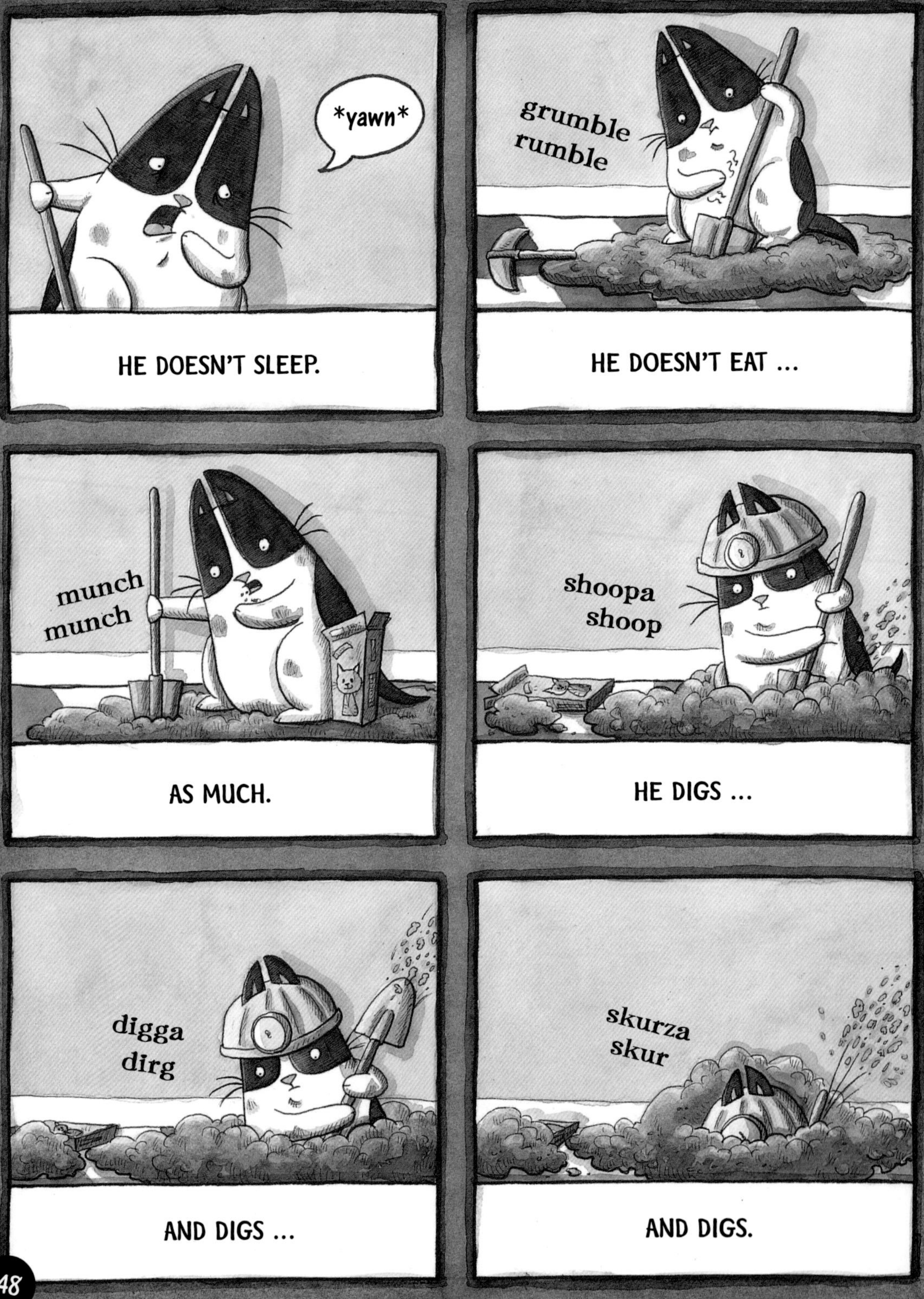
yawn
HE DOESN'T SLEEP.
grumble rumble
HE DOESN'T EAT ...
munch munch
AS MUCH.
shoopa shoop
HE DIGS ...
digga dirg
AND DIGS ...
skurza skur
AND DIGS.

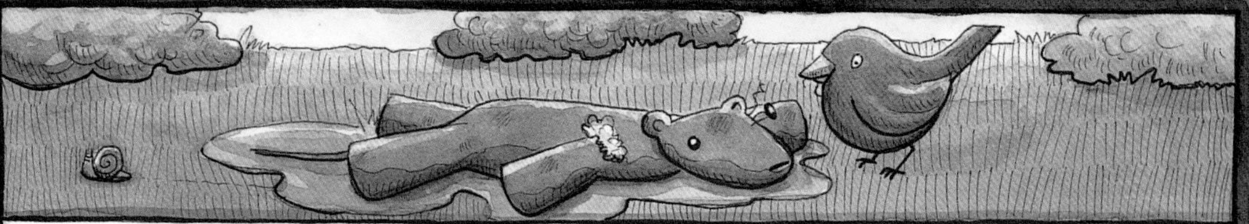

HIS ONLY THOUGHT IS TO SAVE POOR TED.

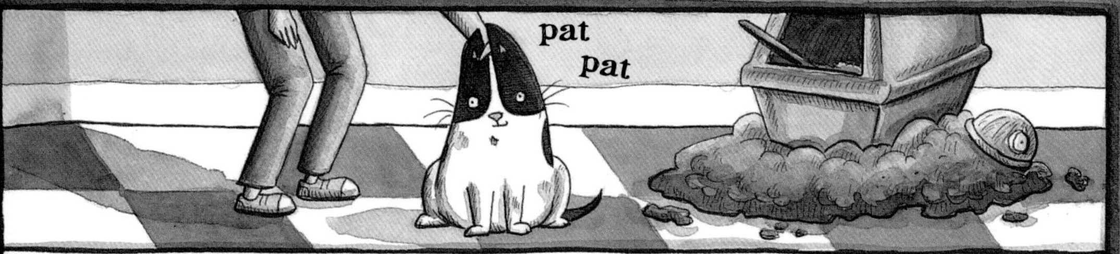
pat
pat

JUST AS HE EXPECTED, HIS HUMANS DON'T NOTICE A THING.

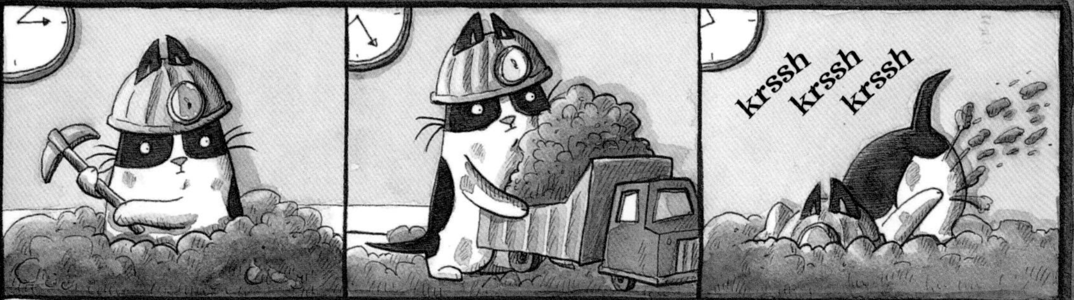
krssh
krssh
krssh

EVEN WORKING AROUND THE CLOCK ...

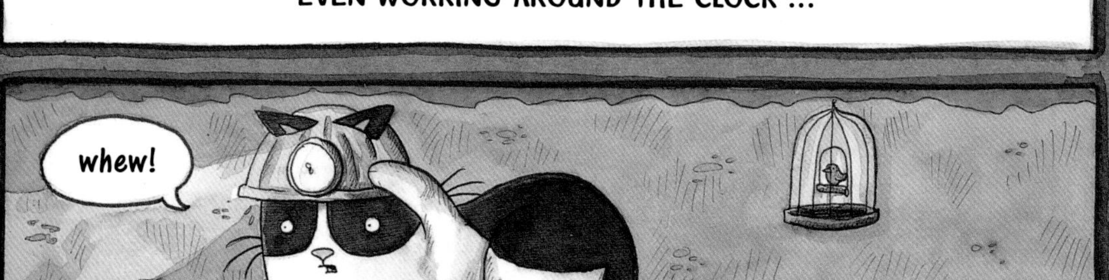
whew!

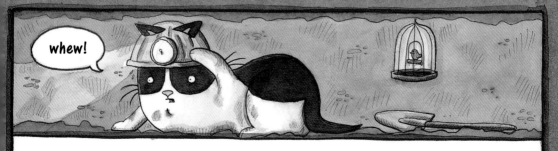

IT TAKES BINKY DAYS TO COMPLETE HIS TUNNEL.

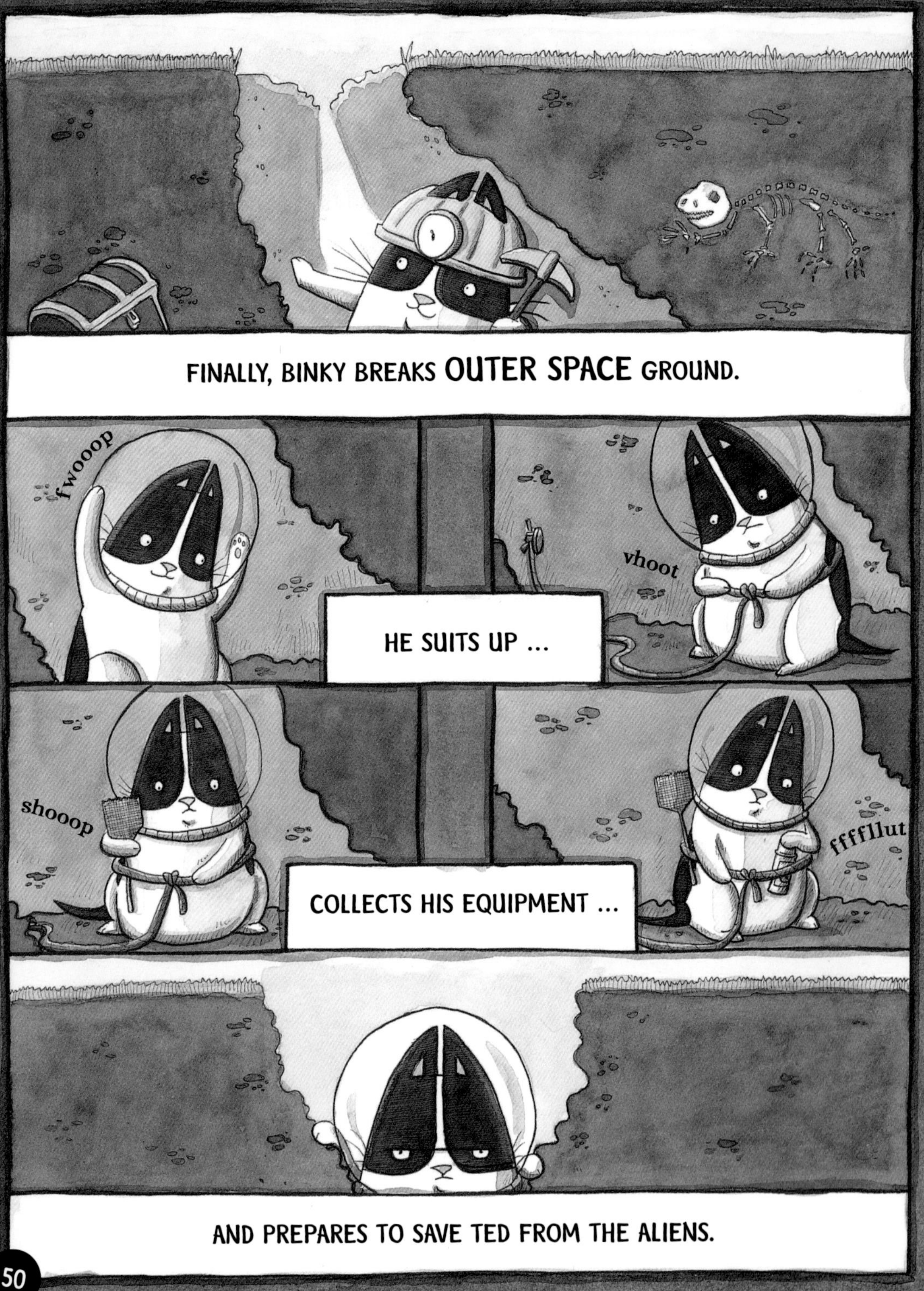
FINALLY, BINKY BREAKS OUTER SPACE GROUND.
fwooop
vhoot
HE SUITS UP ...
shooop
fffllut
COLLECTS HIS EQUIPMENT ...
AND PREPARES TO SAVE TED FROM THE ALIENS.

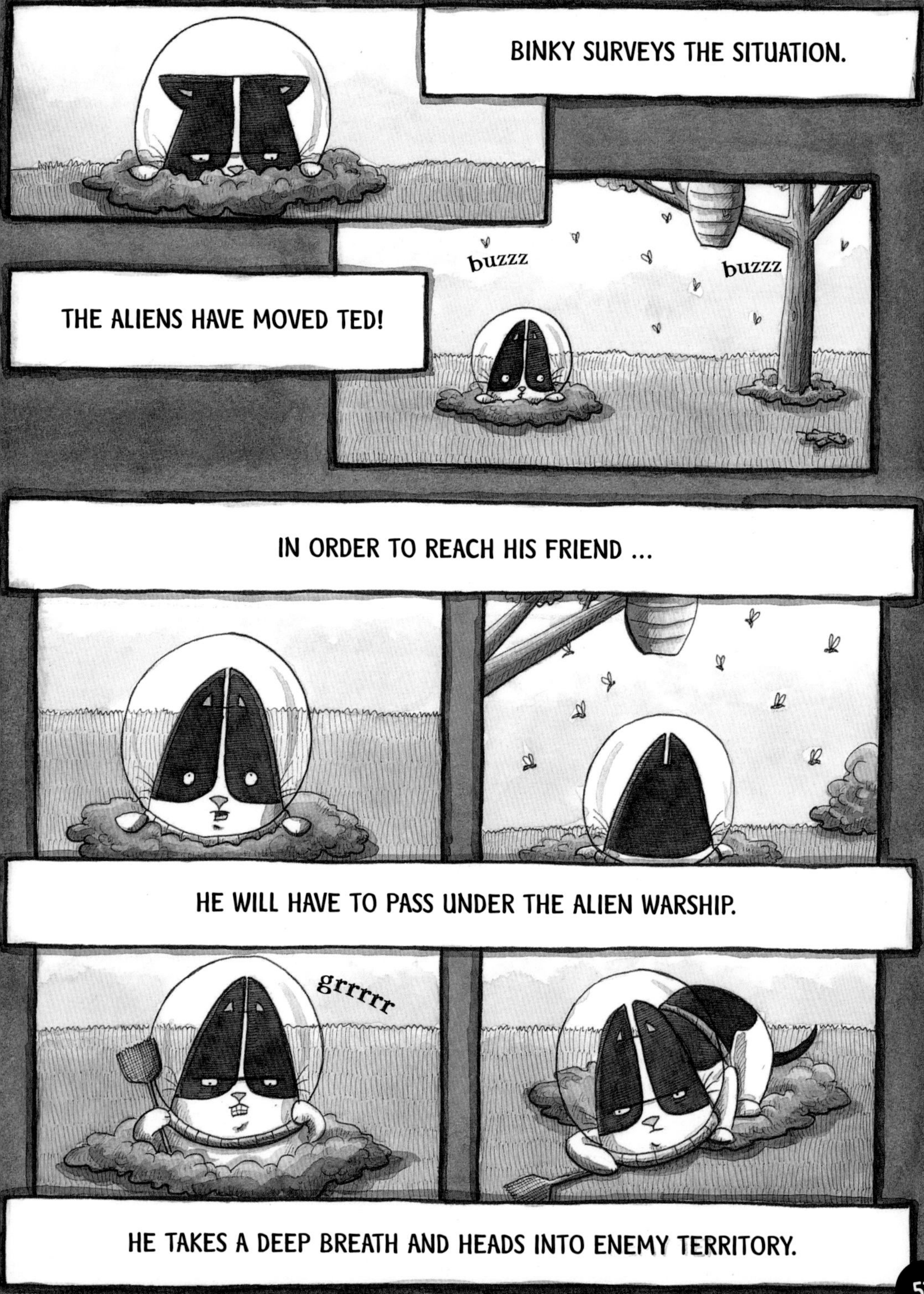
BINKY SURVEYS THE SITUATION.
THE ALIENS HAVE MOVED TED!
buzzz
buzzz
IN ORDER TO REACH HIS FRIEND ...
HE WILL HAVE TO PASS UNDER THE ALIEN WARSHIP.
grrrrr
HE TAKES A DEEP BREATH AND HEADS INTO ENEMY TERRITORY.

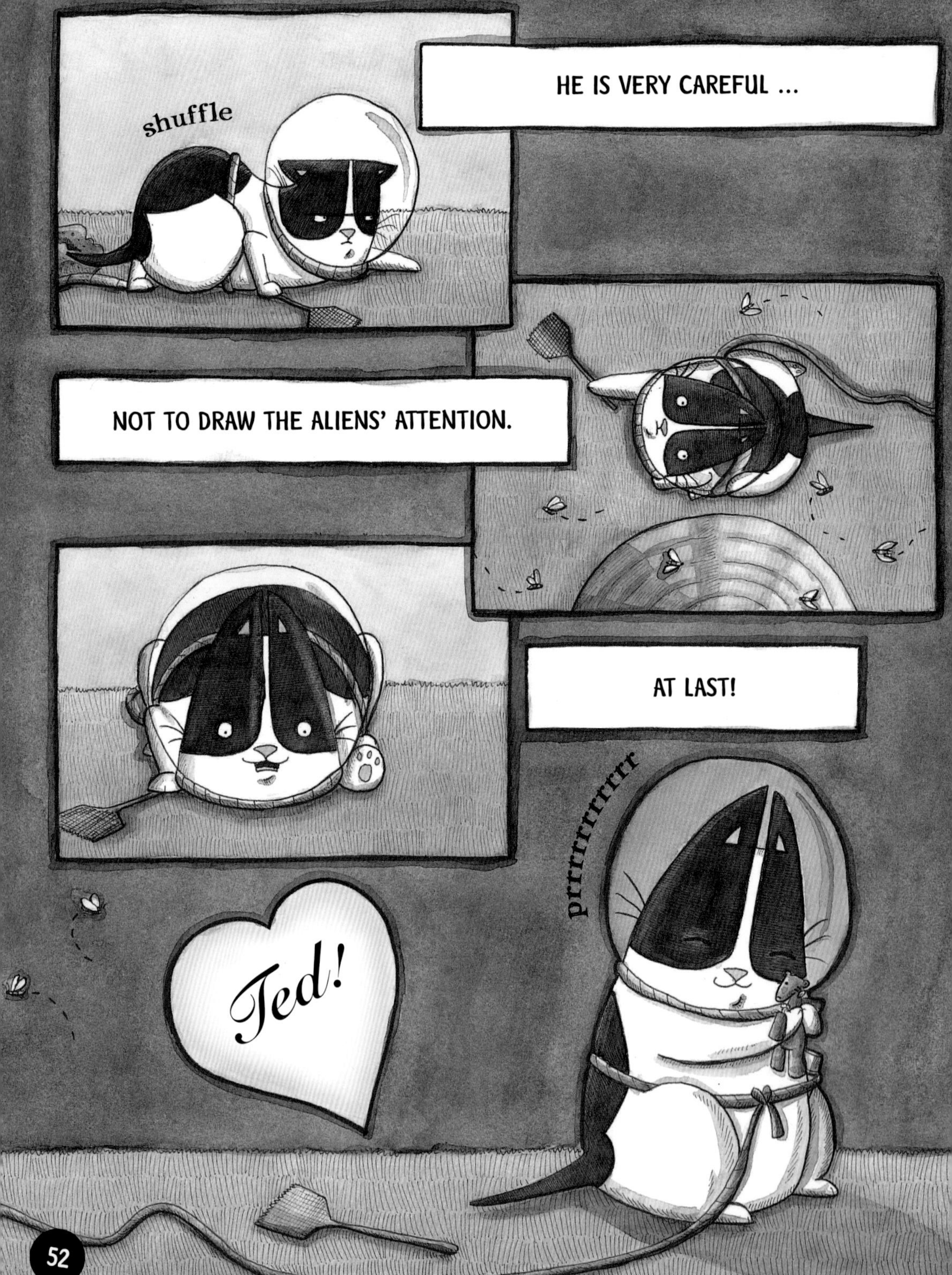
shuffle
HE IS VERY CAREFUL ...
NOT TO DRAW THE ALIENS' ATTENTION.
AT LAST!
Ted!
prrrrrrrrrrr

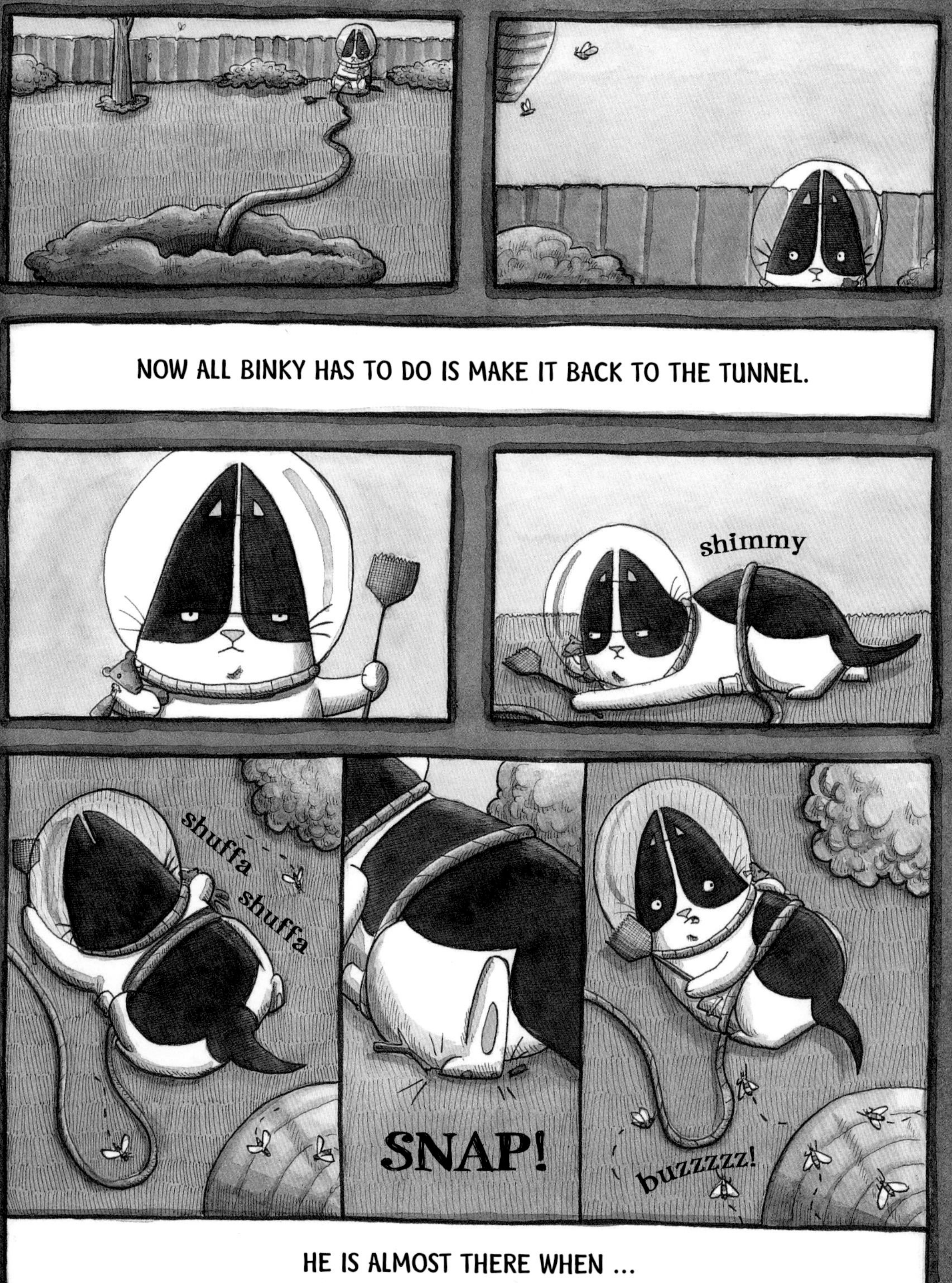
NOW ALL BINKY HAS TO DO IS MAKE IT BACK TO THE TUNNEL.
shimmy
shuffa
shuffa
SNAP!
buzzzzz!
HE IS ALMOST THERE WHEN ...

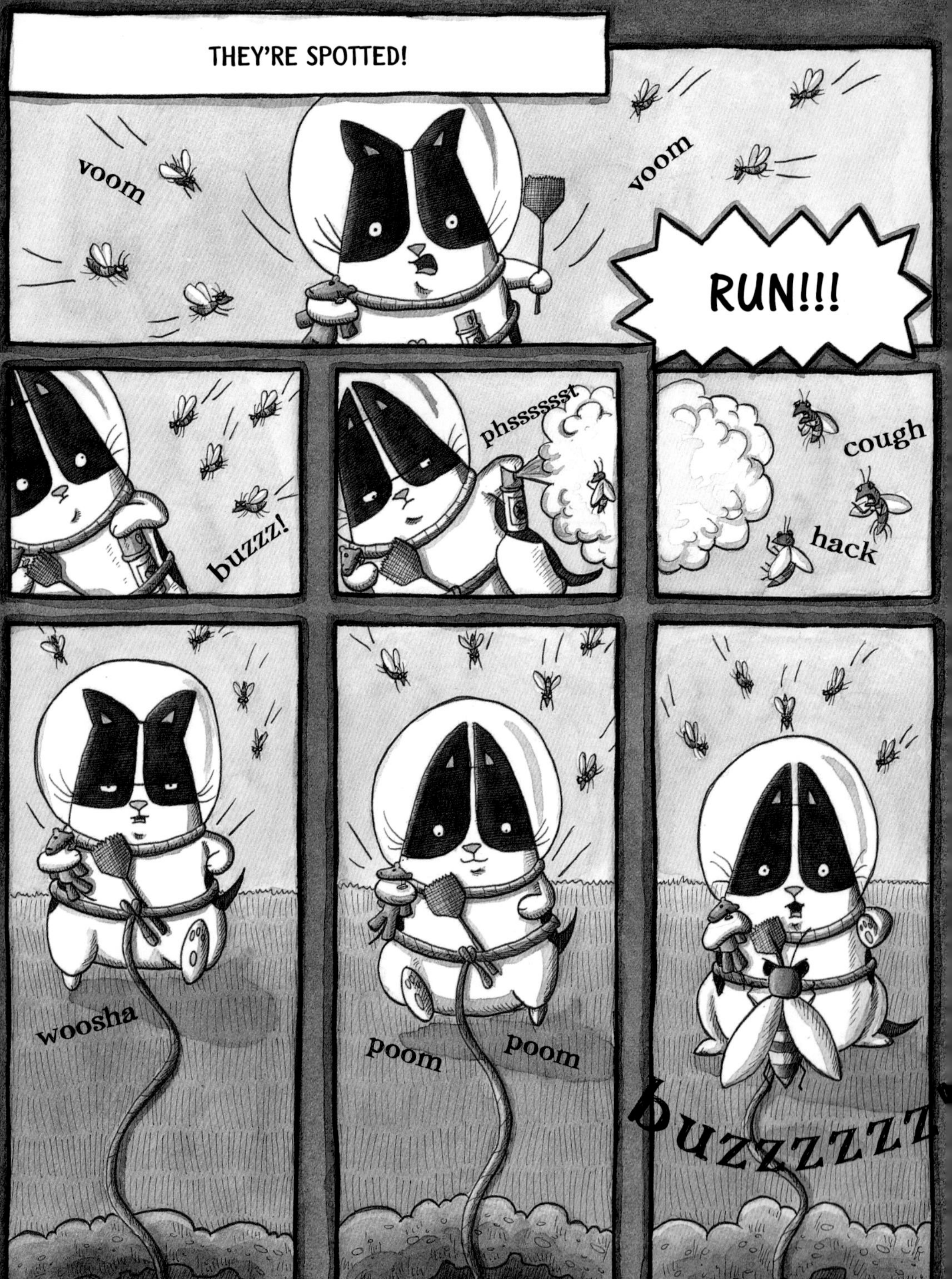
THEY'RE SPOTTED!
voom
voom
RUN!!!
buzzz!
phssssst
cough
hack
woosha
poom
poom
buzzzzzz

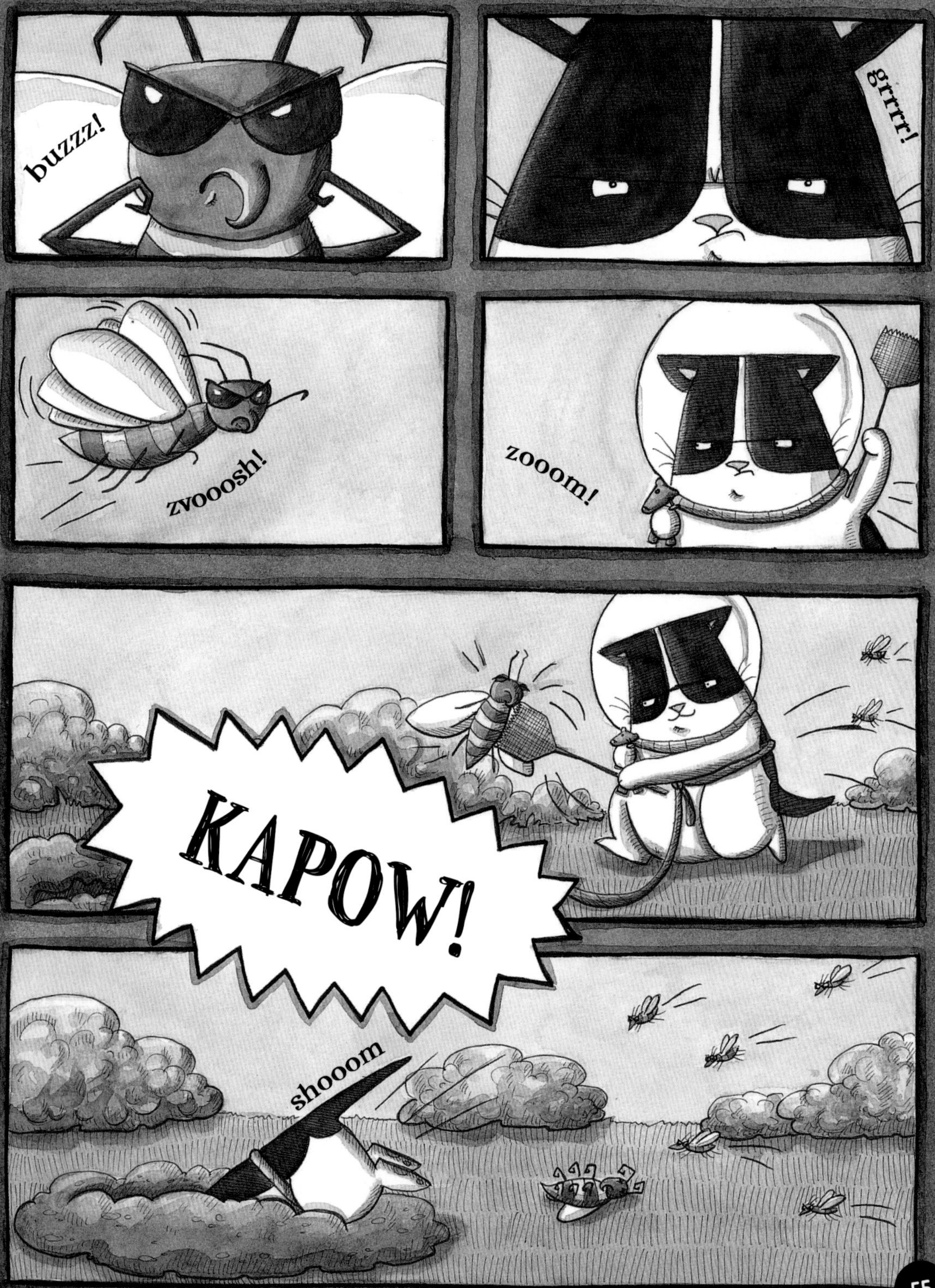
buzzz!
grrrr!
zvooosh!
zooom!
KAPOW!
shooom

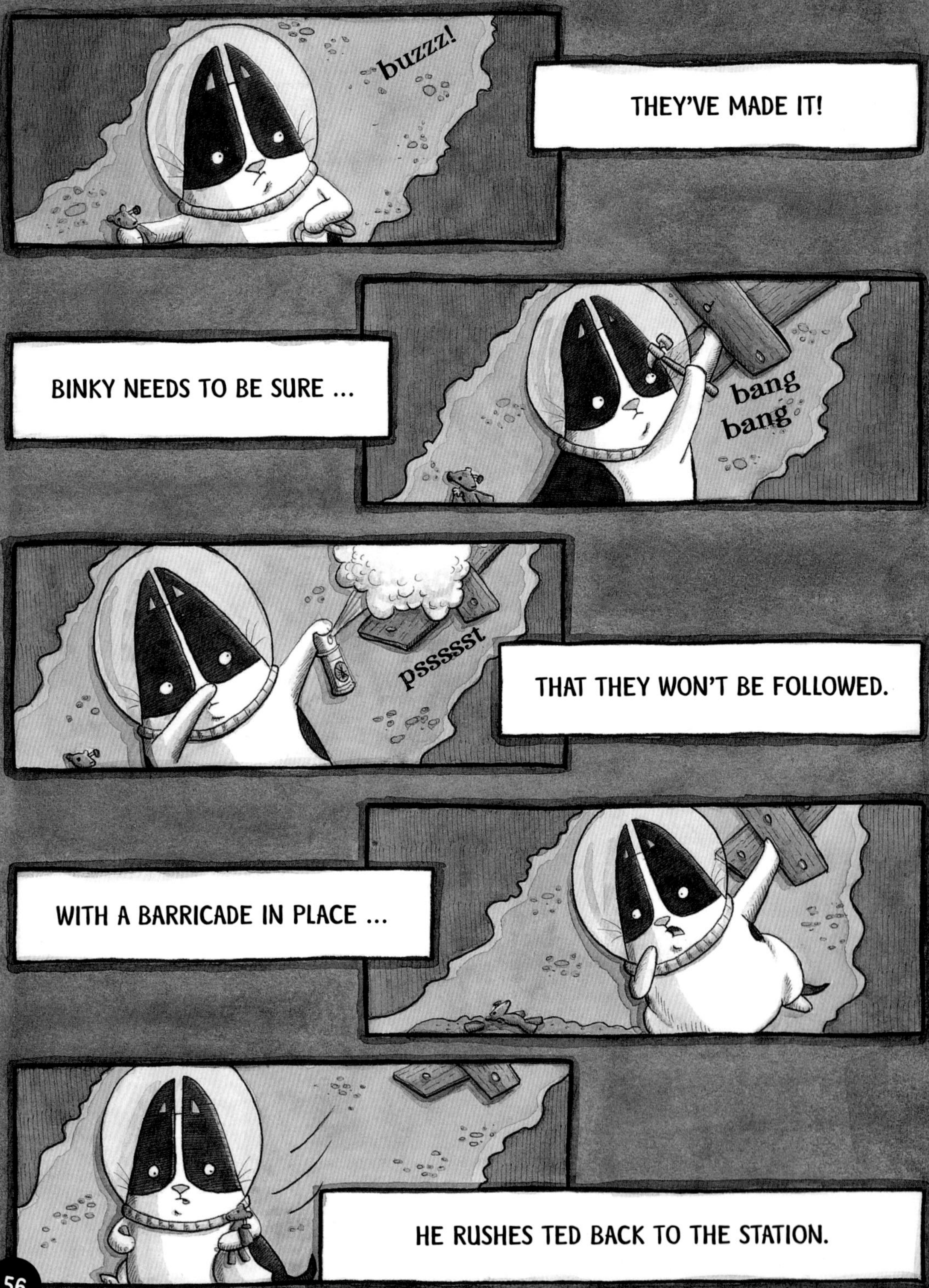
buzzz!
THEY'VE MADE IT!
BINKY NEEDS TO BE SURE ...
bang
bang
pssssst
THAT THEY WON'T BE FOLLOWED.
WITH A BARRICADE IN PLACE ...
HE RUSHES TED BACK TO THE STATION.

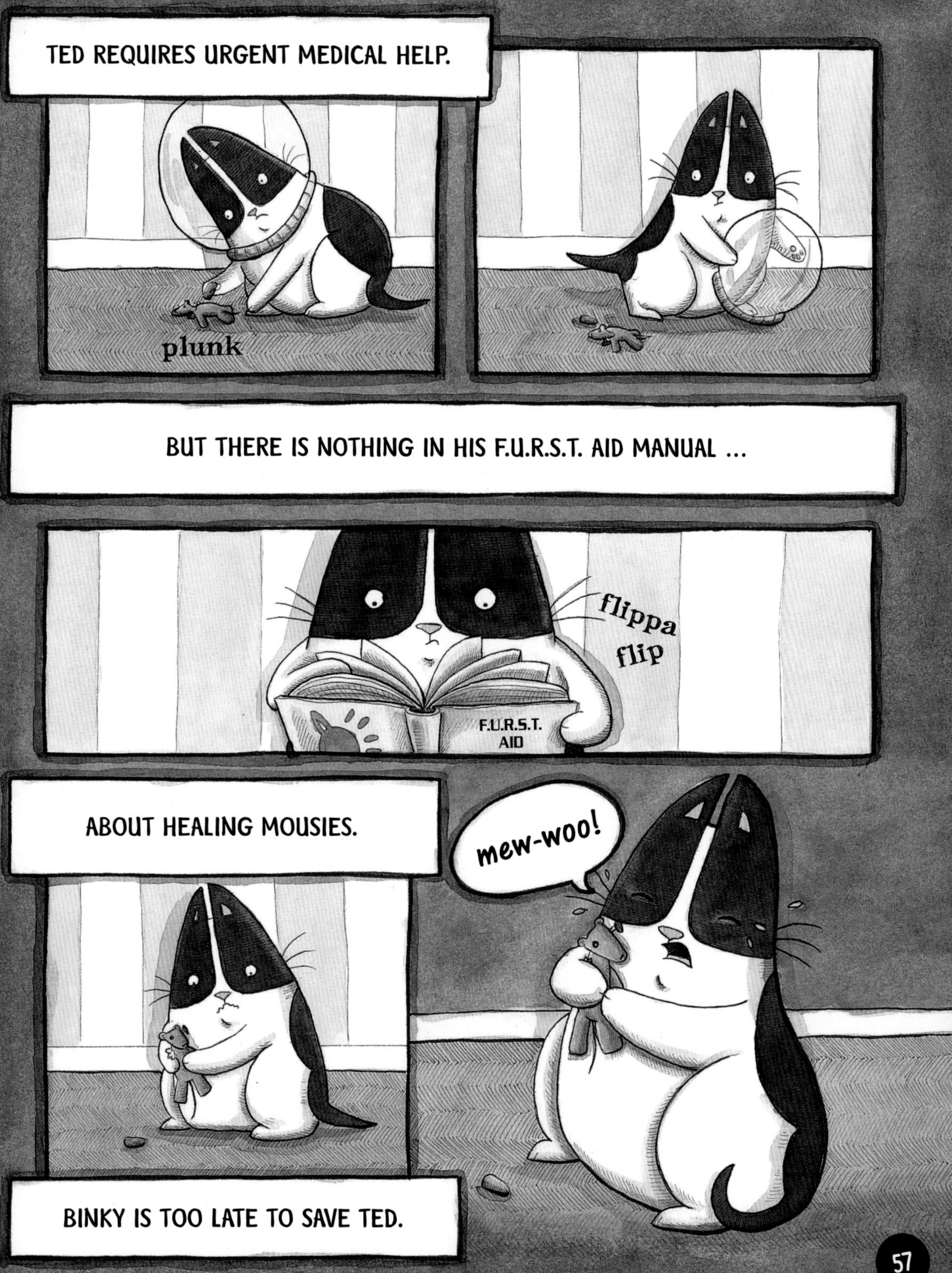
TED REQUIRES URGENT MEDICAL HELP.
plunk
BUT THERE IS NOTHING IN HIS F.U.R.S.T. AID MANUAL ...
flippa
flip
F.U.R.S.T.
AID
ABOUT HEALING MOUSIES.
mew-woo!
BINKY IS TOO LATE TO SAVE TED.

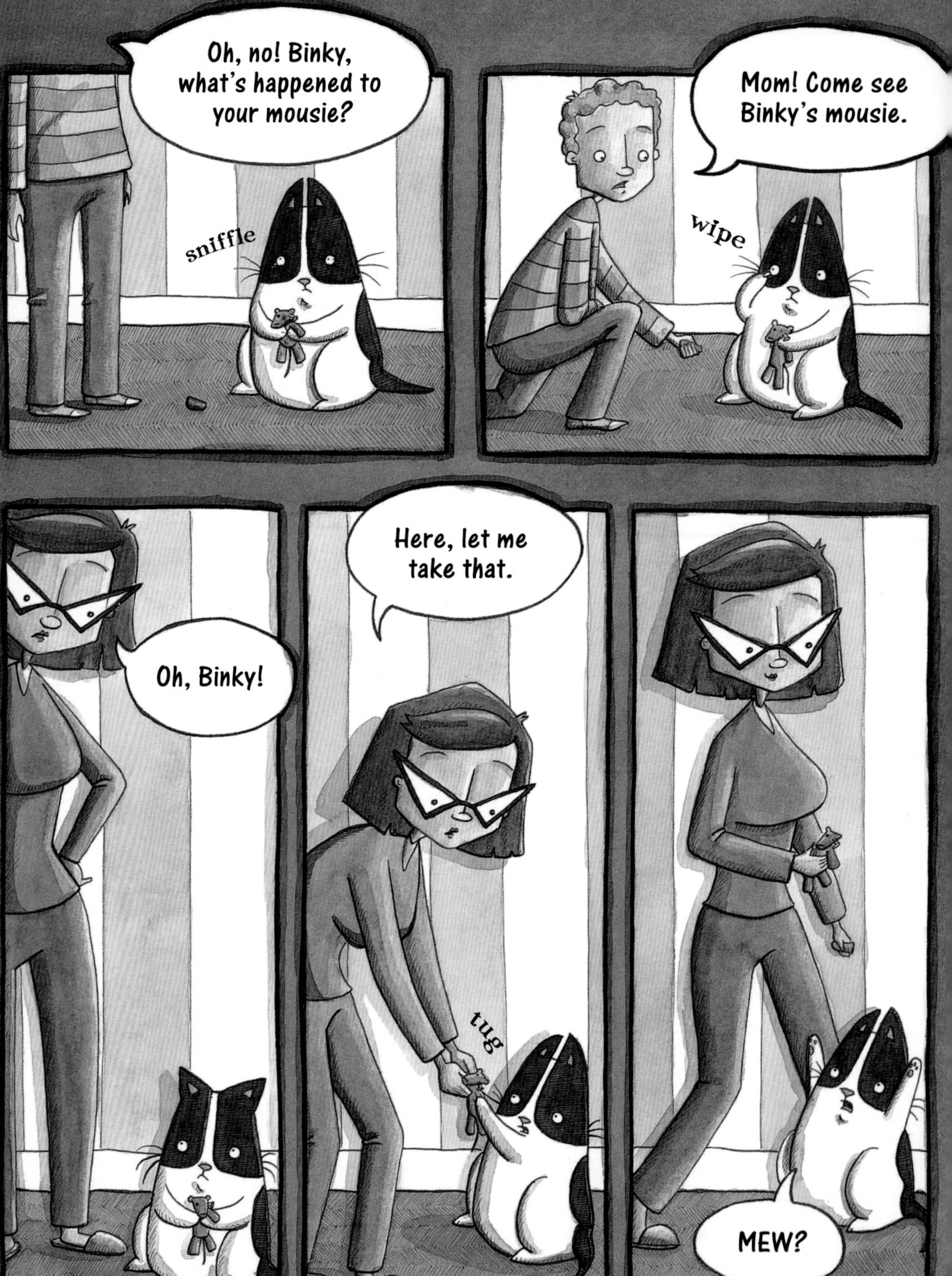
Oh, no! Binky, what's happened to your mousie?
sniffle
Mom! Come see Binky's mousie.
wipe
Oh, Binky!
Here, let me take that.
tug
MEW?

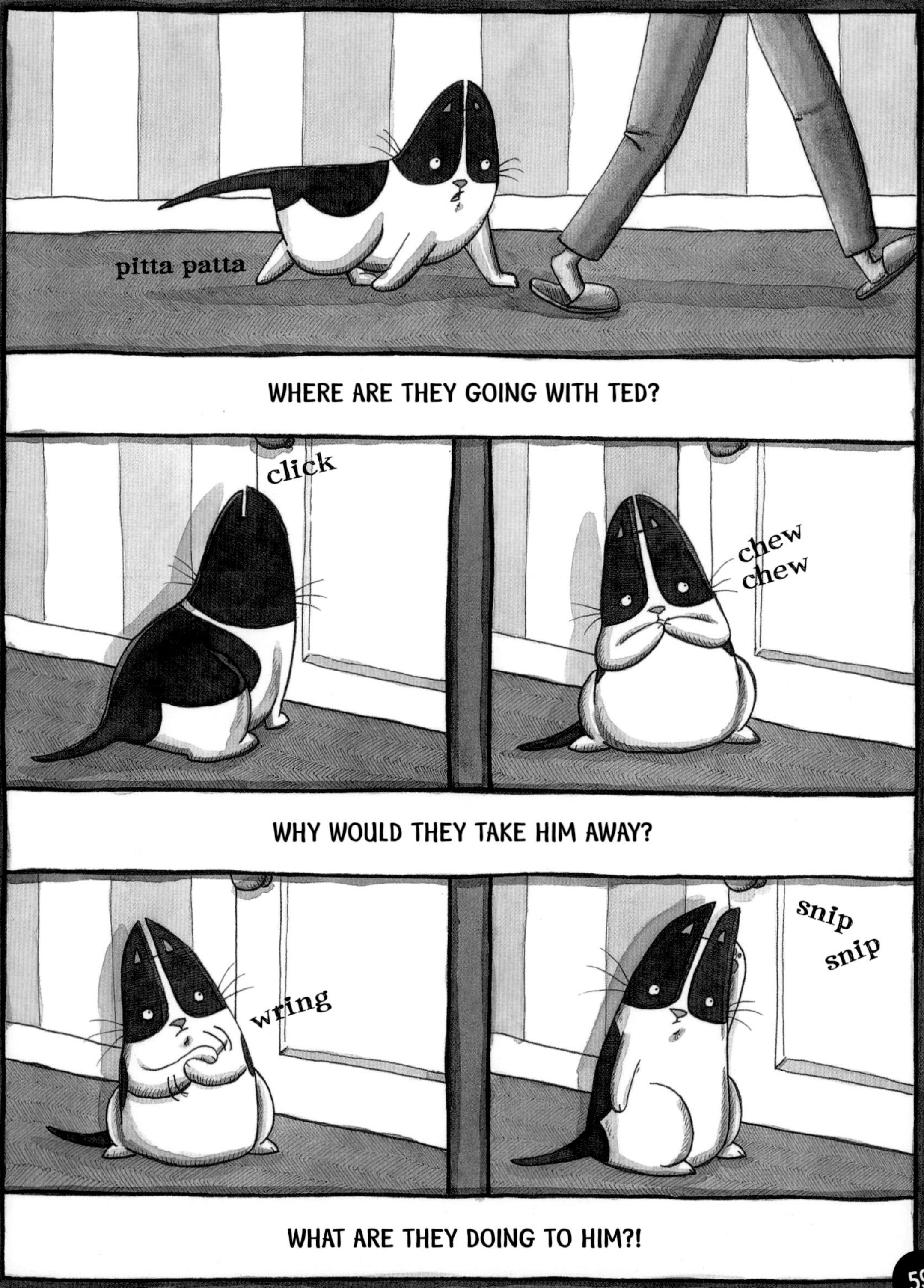
pitta patta
WHERE ARE THEY GOING WITH TED?
click
chew
chew
WHY WOULD THEY TAKE HIM AWAY?
wring
snip
snip
WHAT ARE THEY DOING TO HIM?!

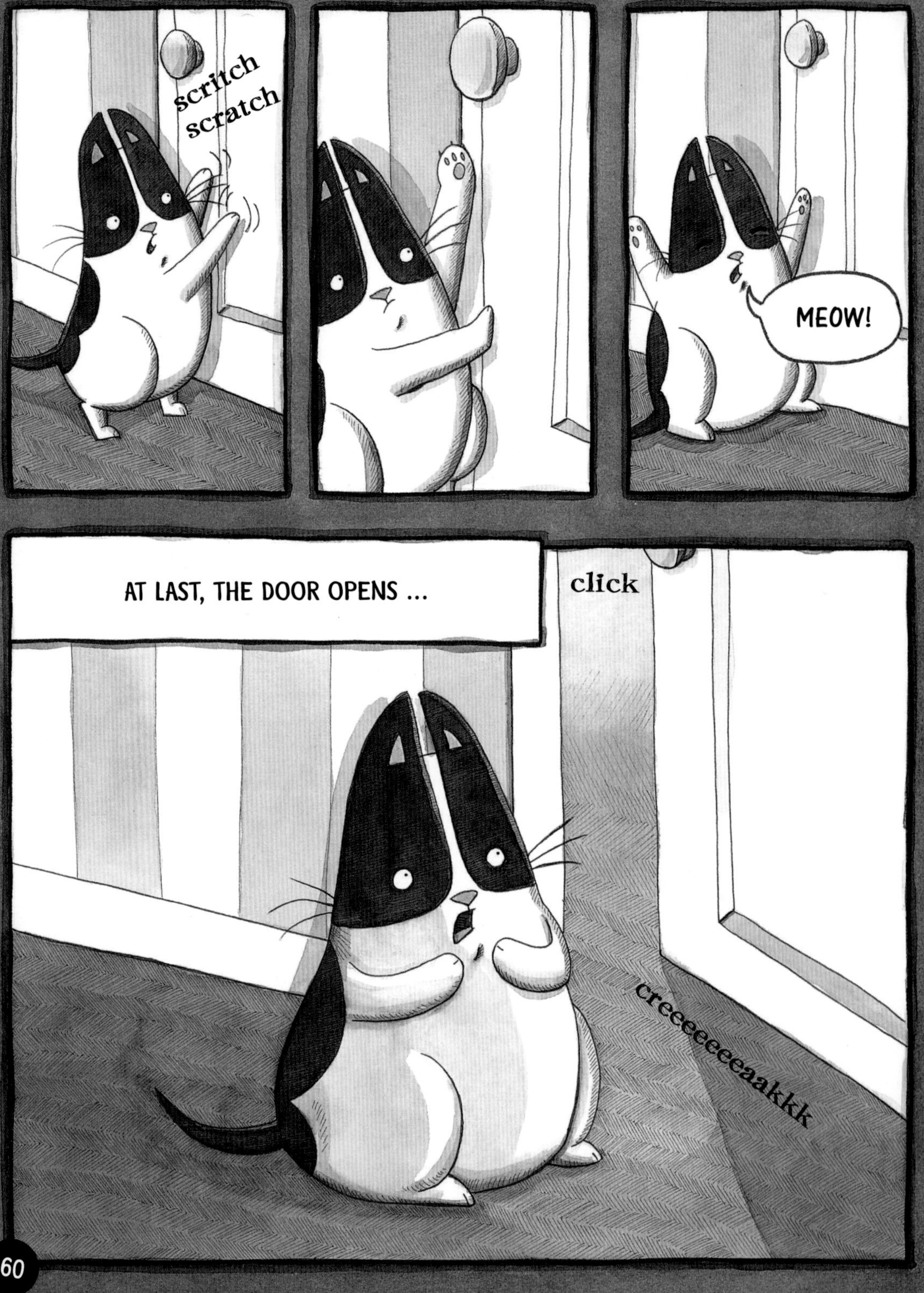
scritch
scratch
MEOW!
AT LAST, THE DOOR OPENS ...
click
creeeeeeeaakkk

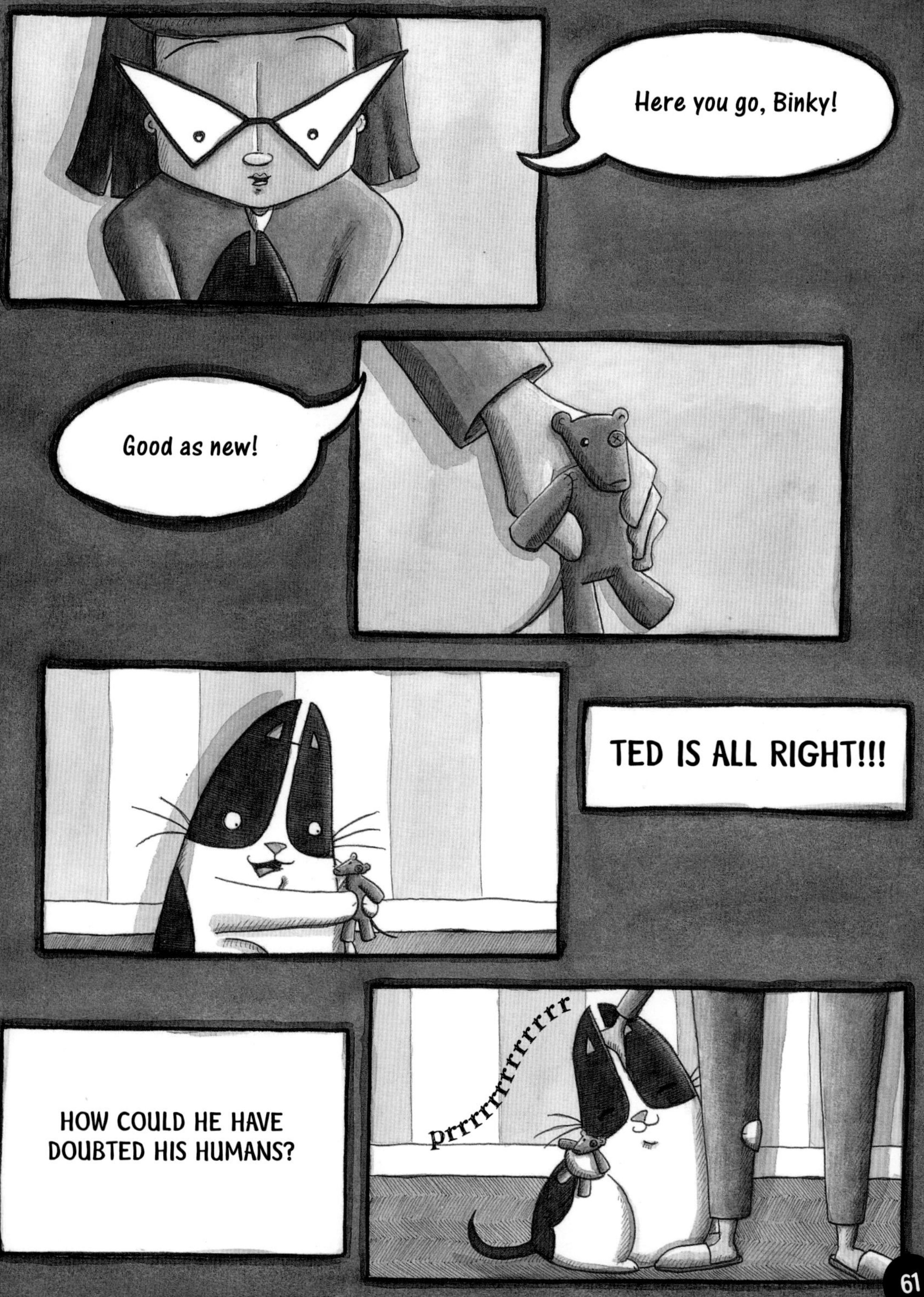
Here you go, Binky!
Good as new!
TED IS ALL RIGHT!!!
HOW COULD HE HAVE DOUBTED HIS HUMANS?
prrrrrrrrrrrrr

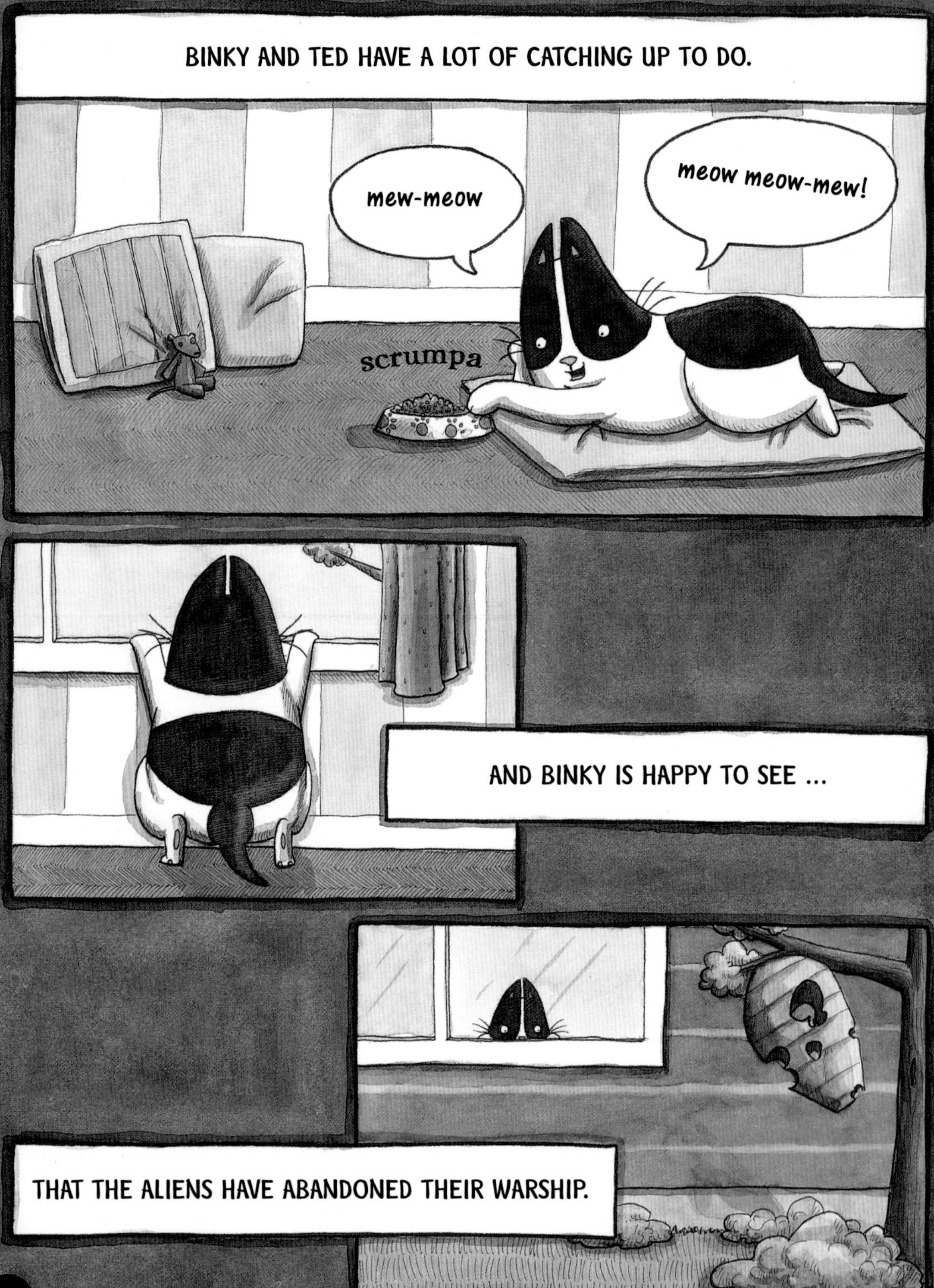

BINKY AND TED HAVE A LOT OF CATCHING UP TO DO.
mew-meow
meow meow-mew!
scrumpa
AND BINKY IS HAPPY TO SEE ...
THAT THE ALIENS HAVE ABANDONED THEIR WARSHIP.

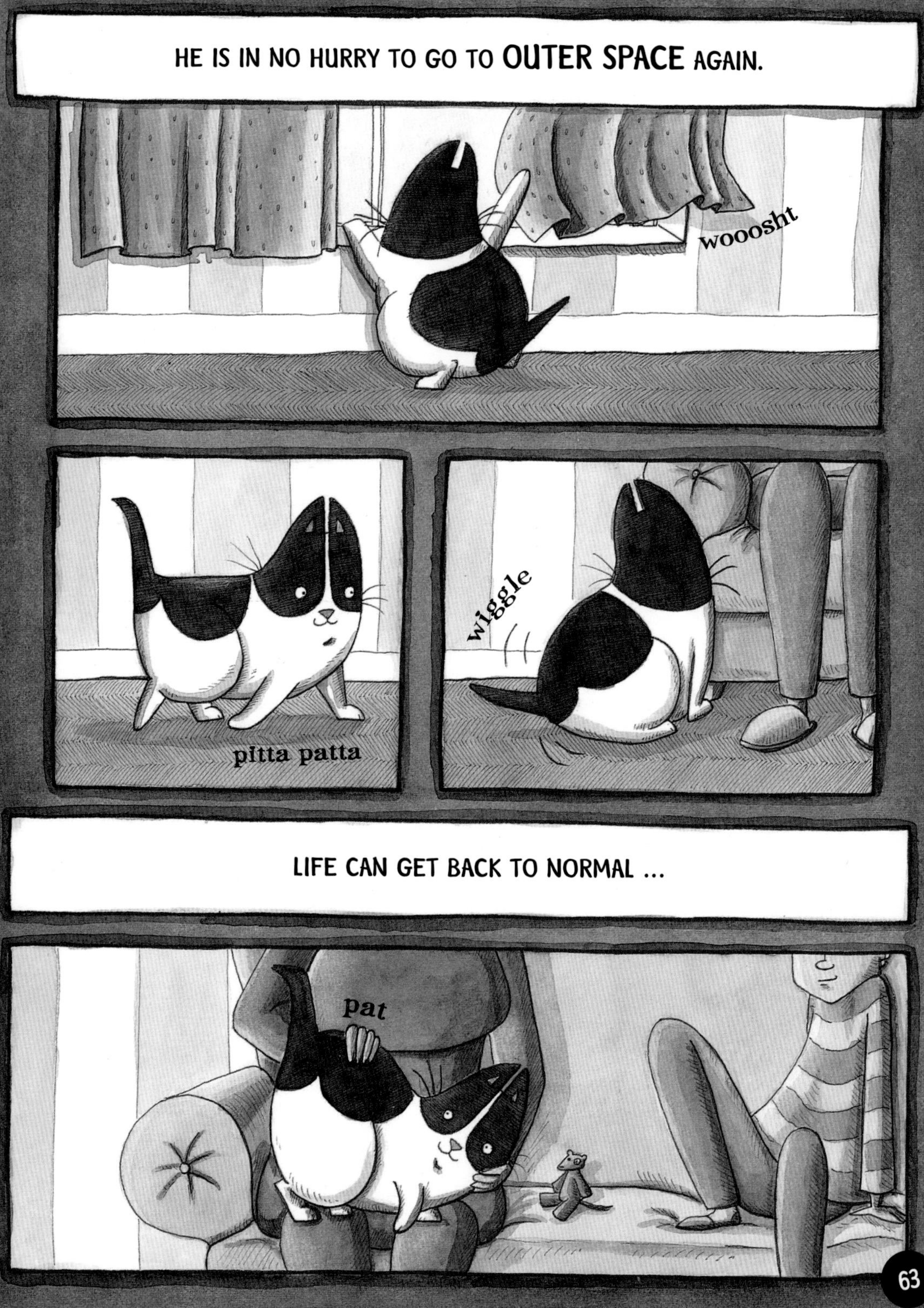
HE IS IN NO HURRY TO GO TO OUTER SPACE AGAIN.
wooosht
pitta patta
wiggle
LIFE CAN GET BACK TO NORMAL ...
pat

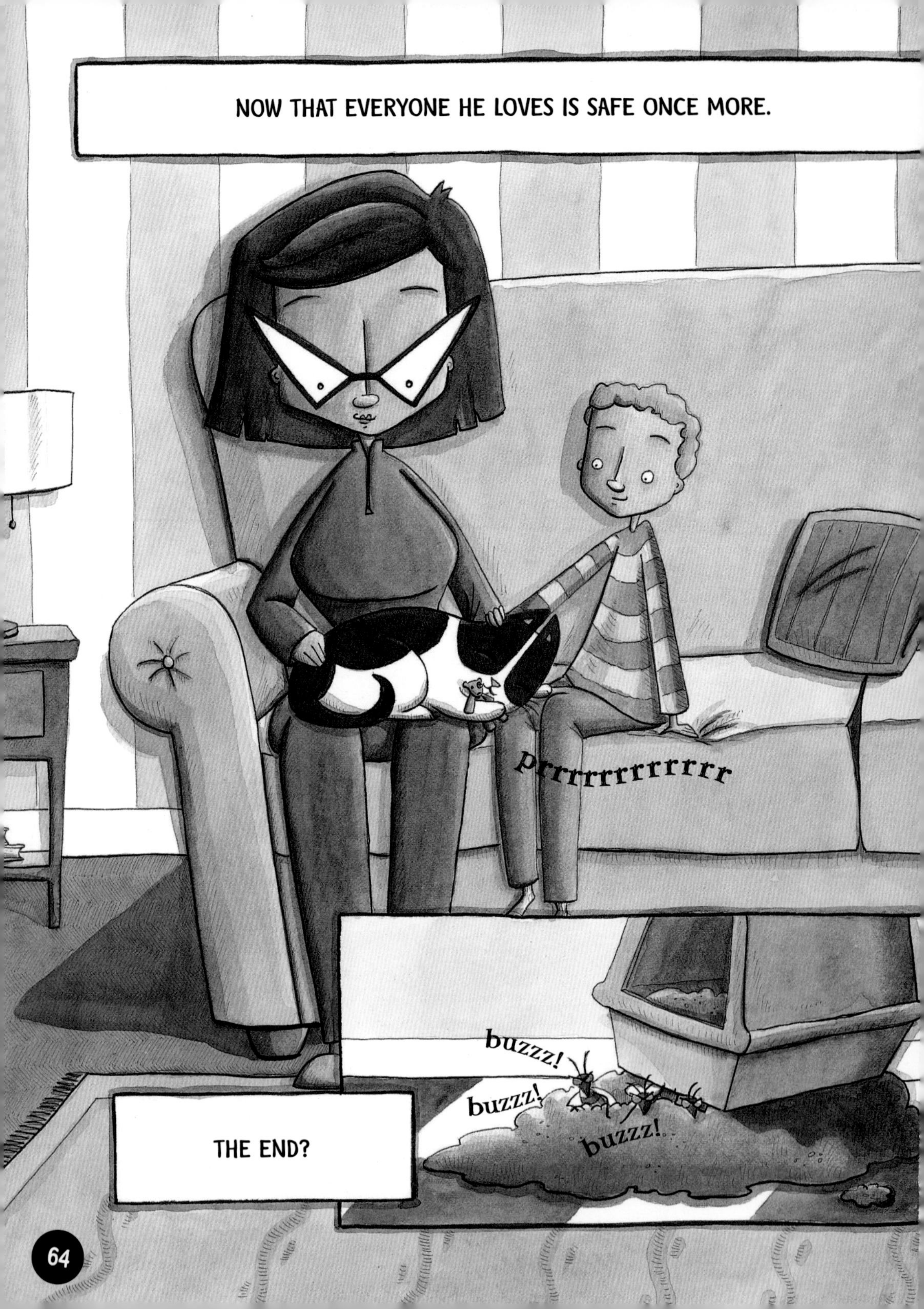
NOW THAT EVERYONE HE LOVES IS SAFE ONCE MORE.
prrrrrrrrrrrr
buzzz!
buzzz!
buzzz!
THE END?